⍟ BODIES 4 SALE ⍟

by

CHARLES NUETZEL

WRITING AS "JOHN DAVIDSON"

The Borgo Press
An Imprint of Wildside Press

MMVII

☙ CONTENTS ❧

☙ INTRODUCTION ☙

I suppose the best place to start would be at the beginning. And supposin' again, that would be *Frozen Smiles & Glad Hands*. Plus a little bow to the fact that this was one of my very first novels, and certainly the first to touch on show business, even in a vague manner of speaking.

Okay, it all started in at piano-bar sometime in the mid-twentieth century, when steak houses were famous for offering, of all things, steak and potatoes as their fame main course at fancy prices. Well, by today's consideration, paying a little under twenty bucks for a couple of top-rate dinners, including cocktails and all the trimmings, plus live music to inspire a romantic mood and…well, they just don't make 'em like they used to. Thank the gods, wherever they may be.

I'm getting off the point.

I had written a short story about a man who played piano in one of the fancy eateries, and had to bang out songs like *Sweet Adeline* so the drunks could try to sing the lyrics in slurring voices that couldn't keep on key. But what he wanted was a break, to become a singer, and when the story opened he was expecting a big named agent to come and listen to him sing a few songs, and maybe sign

5

him up for a Vegas gig. This could be his big break. Of course things didn't happen that way. He was glad-handed and offered generous frozen smiles and ignored by Mister Big, even though the audience was generous in their applause.

I had simply wanted to tell the story of the man's pain and the anguish. You know, an inside look at the horrors of show-biz and the terrible cost in human emotions and—well it wasn't a very commercial bit, but locked in my memory and heart. So, when I was asked to write a novel under some pressure and deadline, I didn't have time to waste, and out came the manuscript *Frozen Smiles & Glad Hands* as a starter. That gave me Manny Anson. All I had to do, now, was to set up some main character and give him some desperate goals and background, then let the characters tell their story

I picked an actor who had once been on the fast lane of success, only to have it yanked out from under him. All I needed then was your standard everyday females tossed into the plot! The stew was beginning to boil hot!

Just like that I had the beginnings of *Bodies 4 Sale*, which takes a bold look at the seedy side of show business, the Hollywood parties, the prostitutes and big money managers.

Jim Norton knew show business from top to bottom. Once he'd been on top and now was at the rock bottom. He never knew what really happened.

And that's where I picked up my characters and started to stir them around.

It was published by Epic Novels back in 1961, and then translated in Europe. Now updated, it tells the story of what it is like to be famous in a town that cares about nothing other than success, big bucks, and fame means knowing the right people to keep you on top! Even if they might have had underworld connections.

Okay, to say more would simply spoil the plot. It all starts south of the border, down Mexico way...

—CHARLES NUETZEL
Thousand Oaks, California
July 2006

BODIES 4 SALE, BY CHARLES NUETZEL

⚲ ONE ⚲

"Hey, honey, what's keeping you so long?" the rasping voice of the whore moaned in the background. Norton didn't respond at first. He was looking at himself in the mirror.

You have an ugly puss! He cursed inwardly. He didn't really believe it, but the way he was feeling right then, he didn't care.

"You gonna stay there all night?" the woman demanded.

He watched her nude reflection in the mirror. She had a fairly good body for a pick-up. Large brown breasts, which were rigidly tipped with erect nipples. Her stomach was large and a little fat, but that was normal for a Latin. Long, heavy thighs and legs. Not like Lilly Benton, but that was another subject he didn't want to think about right then.

She squirmed a little, letting her hand run along her chest. "Come on, what's you doing?"

He gripped the dresser to keep his balance. That last damn drink was getting to him. And he needed drinks badly—much too badly during the last couple of years.

Two years on the downgrade. That was a laugh. This was the mid-twentieth century, and not a time to be without funds. Actually, two years completely

9

flat—bumming around Mexico and South America, but not actually seeing the countries, only the whoring sluts that each nation had to offer. They were all the same. Wiggling, squirming, biting little tramps that would let a man have them for the price of a bottle of booze.

Just like this one!

What was he complaining for? He'd been getting enough women.

He reached for the half-filled quart of whiskey that was on the dresser in front of him. His eyes couldn't help noticing the anxious dark body of the woman behind him. She was still looking at him in a strange way, her eyes frowning and her mouth pouting.

"Aren't you ever coming on over here?" she pleaded, stroking herself in a frantic effort to soothe the heated excitement which she apparently felt so strongly inside her.

At least she wasn't some cheap, bloody whore. Just a hot lady out to get her a man for the night. Obviously wanting it bad enough to make the bar scene.

Wasn't he ever coming over there? That was a question that Lilly Benton had asked, just last week. Lilly Benton, big-time movie queen who had not only been his leading lady in pictures but also managed to share a good portion of his love and life while making the film. Well that had all happened while he was still *on top.*

"Wasn't he ever coming over on her side?" Lilly had wanted to know. "Look, it's a good deal! All you have to do is see this guy Williams—it's real solid, believe me!"

10

So he'd believed her and gone to meet this SOB. Mr. Williams, triggerman for a big shot gangster. They had a real hot deal set up for her—and tomorrow he was going to see what it was all about. Quick money—made a little illegally. But who cares? Jamie Norton had to have money for booze and women. And money didn't grow on that golden money-tree he'd freely plucked during those Hollywood years.

If Jamie Norton didn't get his drunken way...

"Hell, you fairy-man! Bring a lady up to a hotel room and you don't do her! Hell, you gay? I'm leaving!" The woman started to get up from the bed.

Norton turned, savagely. It wasn't that he really cared about her, or that it was necessary to please her—he simply didn't like what she'd just said.

He moved to her, with a low animal grunt of anger. With one shove he pushed her back on the bed. A startled yell sounded from her, as she eagerly grabbed at him. Without a word he covered her lips with his and cruelly clawed at her breasts and shoulder.

She moaned in delight and her voice ripped past her teeth as the kiss parted for air.

"Come *on*..." she cried, "that's the way I just *love* it!"

Her body convulsively squirmed as he started kissing her throat, then arched up as his lips glided down along her shoulder.

"Yes. That's it!" She moaned, thrashing wildly under his kisses. Her breasts lifted to smother his lips. "Oh, wonderful...!"

She gripped his head, moving him back and forth between her breasts in frantic joy. Moaning

11

replaced words, as she drove him further down. She promptly arched up to meet him with such greedy need that it seemed she would go mad under his kisses.

But even her frantic passion wasn't enough to really smother his own mental confusion about his life and the coming deal with Williams. The whole thing had happened too fast, but procured an easy solution to his current long-standing money problems.

He still hated it. Instinct warned him.

And now this woman was here with him, and the two of them were consuming one another like savage animals trying to escape shadowy demons hiding in the darkness beyond the room.

He wondered what drove her mad hunger.

She went crazy under him, then suddenly she was on top, lips racing over his own hard body. Her hands clawed and her lips devoured with such lustful need that it was finally crushing away all his awareness.

When she suddenly lifted away, his eyes popped open, saw her leaning over him, gazing down in open admiration.

"Oh, you're so...hard...all over..." she moaned, hands tearing at his chest. Then suddenly she clawed at him with skilled fingers and the next thing he knew hot fires bathed through his every nerve and wouldn't let him go in their intense demanding fury.

* * * * * * *

The two men sat in the corner of the dark booth,

talking in low voices.

One was heavy and big looking, the other tall and intelligent, and careful. The tall one was talking in a half whisper.

"What I want is to see Delcado out of the way...I don't care how you do it. We don't like the set-up he's beginning to work on. Get me?"

The other nodded and then asked. "What about the Norton guy? I'm supposed to contact him tomorrow for the job!"

"If he comes in, he gets it, too. Understand?"

"Right between the eyes! A...38 bullet will do it every time!"

"With Delcado out of the way, you can do what you want. Take over—just so that you are willing to cooperate with the Vegas boys...we didn't want any more smart guys running the show here in L.A."

"When do I do the job?"

"Play along for awhile. We'll tell you when to blow the deal. It won't be too long!"

The other just nodded silently.

"Don't do anything until we call you—got me Williams?"

Williams just smiled, stood and then left. The other man stayed where he was for a long time, drinking one more cocktail and then he went outside to a car that was waiting for him. One hour later he was flying back to Las Vegas in his own private plane.

* * * * * * *

Norton looked nervously at the bald-headed man sitting at the end of the bar, and felt that same fearful grind of panic he had experienced the first time he had ever really given any serious thought to the matter of coming in on this crooked deal

The drinks he'd had at the apartment where he'd just left the whore had helped some, but now he needed one more strong jolt, and there wasn't any way to get it except by stepping up to the bar where Williams was now seated, silently waiting.

This was the final moment of decision. Did he want a life of being a no good bum or did he want plenty of money and plenty of high class women—Hollywood starlets who would give their bodies to any man that might help their careers?

Hating himself, Norton made his decision, without much serious consideration.

He walked up to the bar and his new career, sat down beside the smaller man and extended his hand.

"How are ya?" he greeted, his face creasing with a forced smile. His stomach muscles tightened in order to hold down the contempt and sick feeling that was churning there. He didn't like this man—or anything to do with the bastard—except the guy's money.

And money he needed.

Williams slowly turned and looked carefully at Norton.

"You look pretty good for a bum." the man grumbled, ignoring the extended hand.

A short silence followed, while their eyes held contact.

The man continued with: "You decide to play ball? Lil was right about you, then."

Norton wanted to ram the guy's teeth down his throat and make him choke on them. But this wasn't

14

the time to show any sign of temper—or unleash the kind of emotion that had ruined him with his agent, Manny Anson.

"You gonna buy me a drink, bum?" Williams requested, smiling briefly.

It was a command, not a suggestion or question. A gentle command, to see how far he could push his "new boy." The only trouble was that the man could push Norton just as far as he wanted. The money the guy represented was too important. Norton had been living too high when he was on top and now that his funds were dwindling down to nothing, he could be pushed as hard as anybody wished to push him, as long as they paid his price.

In two years he'd fallen that far.

"What you drinking?" he inquired, holding down the inner anger which still wanted to snap back at this little slob!

"Scotch and water."

Norton called the bartender over and ordered for the two of them. He needed a drink, badly. A good strong one. Something to keep the bitter taste of anger from surfacing.

If it weren't for Lilly…

Lilly had stuck her neck out for him and the only thing that he could now really do was to try to deal his cards smart, for a while, at least. That was the trouble with show business and the whole world. Somebody tried to help you and, then, after it was too late, you were the one who had to see the deal though. If it weren't for his inner hunger for money and fame he wouldn't be in this trap. And that was a serious problem for him. Once show business was in his blood, his addiction to it developed stronger and

15

stronger until it was an emotional drug he couldn't live without. You had to have the food for your sickness—show business, fame and money and women.

The only problem with him was that he never had any real talent. He'd climbed up the ladder through a series of accidents and help from his one-time agent. Manny had created and promoted Jamie Norton from a nobody to a big time somebody. Then later back to a nobody. Manny had made him and then broken him with no more effort than it took to snap his fingers.

Bloody damned agents. Bloody damned power brokers.

Manny had said, over and over that talent meant nothing: "If you have a good cameraman, good lighting man, good director and film editor, well, you don't need a highly trained actor with talent bursting out of his pores. Talent is cheap in Hollywood. It is all promotion. Good bodies are cheap, too. And, sure, you have a good one! The women want to paw you naked and get what you have between your legs between theirs! That's what we sell in films. And putting you into a flick is nothing more than deal-making! Has nothing to do with your...talent or lack thereof!"

Williams' voice broke. Into his thoughts then, "I asked you, are you ready to take off?"

"What? To where?"

"Look, either you're with us or you're not. We don't have no more time to waste. So? Are you ready to leave this hell pit and come back to the States?"

"What if I say 'no'?"

16

"Then it's goodbye to a sweet smelling deal! All the hot broads spreading their legs for your...stud act. They'll whimper to get you in bed! That's what you want, isn't it? That and money. And out of this crappy life you've been sucking up to down here south of the boarder!"

"What if I decide to call in the police?"

Williams looked at him in such a startled way that Norton was almost shocked by the guy's reaction: "You do that, and buddy, you'll end up in the river or ocean and never find your way back to the surface! Got me?"

He got the guy all right. He got him good!

Williams looked at him hard and piercingly. The stare was cold and unemotional. It didn't ask, it demanded. Either—Or! "Make up your mind, bum! We don't got all day. Gotta get moving. The Big Man wants to see you—fast!"

"You haven't told me anything about the deal!"

"Delcado wants to tell you that!"

"Look, you tell me something or I walk out, right now!"

An amazed expression shook Williams' features and for a short moment a sign of minor respect. "Okay, this much I can tell you: two night clubs— one on the Sunset Strip, and another out on 101 Highway just outside of Santa Monica. Both with your name on them. The 101 set-up is supposed to have a private club where a little gambling will be going on—got me?"

He got it! And he didn't know how much he liked it.

"Now that's it. You come or you go. I don't care which—but make up your mind—*fast!*"

The man's eyes silently added: *Asshole!*

There wasn't anything he could do. He needed the money. And much to his surprise, the deal wasn't quite as bad as he had thought it might be. Illegal—but it could have been a lot worse.

Williams gulped the rest of his drink and stood.

"This isn't no patty-cake party that we are going to start. It's Big Business. So, are you in?"

Norton felt a knife twist inside him, making his whole body momentarily sick. For only a moment he wished it were possible to back out. But he knew that he was sunk. There was no way out for a man who is weak and starved for the food of his weakness: money and fame. He was too old to really have to start some other business. Show biz was the only thing he knew.

"You sure you want it? Once we start, the boys won't take 'no' for an answer!"

"I'm sure of it!"

"Okay, let's get out of this dive," Williams ordered, pushing him forward. "There's a private plane waiting to take us out of Mexico and to Delcado's home."

The two of them moved across the room, Norton paid the bill; and they left the saloon and stepped out into the dirty street. First to his hotel room and then...

Where?

☙ TWO ❧

Mr. James D. Delcado was a large man, large like his house. Beefy. Thick red features that puffed out his face. Heavy hands. He was a man who held power in those hands and was used to using that power for his own means and desires and passions. A man who could make or destroy any person with a flick of his fingers. A man who would not be pushed or dangled or crossed.

A few moments before, Norton had been ushered into a large room, which was a cross between study, business office and play room. Then he was introduced to his host, after which the big man had ordered everybody out except his guest.

"Jamie Norton! I'm glad to see you came around to our way of thinking!" the man exploded, moving toward the huge bar in the corner of the room.

"I see you're a man after my own heart!" Norton exclaimed, trying to create a lighter mood. For some reason it was hard to think of this otherwise cheerful atmosphere as being anything except as icy cold as Delcado's eyes.

"What'll you have, my boy?" the larger man asked, moving his arms with awkward ease of a gigantic ape. His face seemed to loom across the large bar, and the thin mustache didn't hide the twisted sag of his white narrow lips. There was no doubt about the complete confidence this man felt in his power over others. Every action showed it. The bold tone of his voice accented it. The stone ice of his eyes backed it up like a frosted north wind.

This was the man who now owned Jamie Norton, body and. soul.

"Make mine Scotch," Norton requested.

"Good! Damn good! That's the kind of a drink a man should order!" Delcado placed two glasses on the bar. Ice was dropped into them and a moment later the Scotch flowed into the crystal containers. Then his host pointed to one of the drinks. "Help yourself!"

"Pretty good," Norton commented, after sipping the golden liquor.

"Pretty good, the man says? Pretty good!" Delcado shouted at the air. "You mean that this is damn good Scotch! The best! I have to have it flown in special from Scotland. Have an interest in the company. Always like to have some interest in everything—especially when I like the product." He laughed, showing his teeth, which were uneven and stained; they gleamed as his lips slid back away from them. The laugh was coarsely loud. A noisy, grating, nerve-shattering sound.

Just then the door opened and a beautiful, tiny redhead walked in.

"Hey, honey, what's keeping my little baby doll?"

The woman was dressed in pedal pushers, which clung so tight that Norton was sure that he could see everything she had. Her sweater was fighting against the firm, point breasts. She had a youthful, trampish look about her.

"What you doing here?" Delcado cried, turning savagely toward her. "I told you never to come in here when I'm busy!"

The girl noticed Norton for the first time. That one quick look she gave him was enough to heat the entire north and south poles put together. It was pure animal fire. And his reaction was more than just heat—it was raw fury. Her eyes gave him the up and down routine that said all there was to say. She was hot; and thought he was, too. Her lips smiled momentarily—and they were just asking for it, as if saying: *Honey, I sure wanna screw you something wild like.*

That's when Delcado's arm swung and his hand slapped violently across her face. A scream of pain shot past her lips and she cringed away from the large man.

Delcado turned back toward him and his lips were smiling almost pleasantly. "I'm sorry about—that."

He shook his head and then said: "Back to business. Now, my boy, have a chair and let's talk things over a bit!" The man lumbered awkwardly to a huge, over-stuffed leather chair and dropped downwards like a gigantic tired elephant. "Now sit! Don't like to see my new boys being nervous or tense."

Norton sat. The chair was opposite the other man. It was uncomfortable. It had been built to make the person sitting in it ill at ease. Delcado had no doubt placed it there for that express purpose. It was good business.

"Well, my boy, tell me something about yourself." A finger stabbed outwards toward him. A demanding fat little sword that cut the air in sharp jerking jabs.

"Nothing much. You must know most of the public side of it. I was in show business several years back," Norton began trying to relax, but finding it impossible. He leaned forward resting, elbow on his legs. "You must know about that, or you, wouldn't be interested in me, now would you?"

Delcado nodded his head slowly in agreement.

"Had a run-in with my agent and walked out on him. Wanted me to do certain things that I didn't agree with. After that it was impossible to get work. Some bastard had put the scare in everybody."

Delcado slowly smiled. The expression broadened into an almost evil looking action of his lips. His eyes became shiny with humor: "I know. I know all about that!"

What the hell could this man know about it? Norton wondered, feeling angry pain stab inside him.

Delcado continued leaning closer. "I want to know something about how you think, how you react to a..."

A phone rang on the desk a few feet away from them.

"Excuse me for a moment." Delcado got up and stepped over to the huge desk. Picking up the phone he turned his back to Norton. "Who is it?" his, voice boomed. "Oh.... I forgot. Didn't realize how late it was. Have him wait. Be through in a moment or so."

He hung up and turned toward Norton, "Later than I thought. I'm a busy man. Doctor says I should take it easy, but don't have time to do that. Too many things, and people, to keep under—well, anyway. I have to learn all about you later. Some other time, when we have...well, when I'm not so busy?

He sat down in the chair again, leaning carefully forward and once more stabbing the air with his finger, accenting every word with a snap-like action of his whole arm. "Right now I'm telling you something about the general outline of what's in store for you and what your job will consist of." His features seemed to be much closer than they really were.

"You're gonna be my front man. I've rigged up a club on the strip. Another one on 101, several miles out from Santa Monica. That's the big one. You'll run both, but this is the one I'm interested in. There'll be two managers who have been in the business for years—but you'll be responsible to me, as they will be to you. You do nothing but run the club part. Manage it. I have another man for the casino: Williams will be in charge there. There'll be one of his boys with you, who will pass on the members of the downstairs private-club and be concerned with that operation. He's your assistant at *that* club.

"You have nothing to do with that part. Your job will be hiring and firing restaurant help and nightclub acts. The experience you had in show business will help with that responsibility. Run the club. You can do it any way you like. Let the manager--assistants handle the whole thing if you want. I don't care how you get results—just get them! As long as there's a good show and we draw the right kind of crowd. Money—people—that's what I want.

We'll take care of the rest. I'm just concerned with having the name *Jamie Norton's Club* on the outside of the building. Okay? *Got me?*"

Delcado stood then, and extended his hand.

Norton followed the example and gripped the other's hand in his. "Understand, completely."

"Williams will fill you in on the details. Tonight you stay here as my guest. Have a party planned. And there'll be plenty of broads. And Hollywood people. You'll probably know most of them."

Norton found himself being ushered out of the room. Everything was happening fast; too fast to let him think things out. But that's the way Delcado seemed to want it.

Yet it all sounded pretty sweet. Too sweet. A good set-up for a guy who wanted money and a chance to get a new start.

From drunken bum to nightclub manager! This was better than being with some cheap whore in some cheap hotel room, drinking cheap booze. He might not have complete control of what *really* took place, but he would be paid for the use of his name, and there would be plenty of time to rebuild his career and life back to the place it used to be. Maybe also help a few friends of his, like he had always wanted to.

George Kayne—there was a guy with a lot of talent on the keyboard and a good set of vocal cords. A musician who had never really been given the right breaks. Maybe we should help George.

Just as he got outside the door he saw Manny Anson walking up to Delcado from across the large hallway leading into the other part of the huge house.

24

Manny Anson! The man who had ruined him!

A tight gripping of his gut made him slightly weak and dizzy. He didn't quite know what to do. The man saw him and smiled pleasantly.

"Hi, Jamie, how're things?" Manny shot over his shoulder he stepped into the room Norton had just left.

Too fast. Things were happening much too fast!

He needed a drink to help him gather his reactions and figure things out.

What the hell was Manny Anson doing here, anyway? And did he fit in? And how? Why?

His head was beginning to spin like a top from the sudden series of shocking surprises. Manny had been the last person he would have expected to find here; and the idea that the guy might be connected in any way with Delcado left him icy cold.

What if the guy did fit in? What would be his reactions then?

Williams waddled up to Norton at that point, interrupting his thoughts. He was suddenly glad to see the man. The nasty, little, power-mad man. A bastard who looked with contempt at everything and everybody. A sharp-tongued individual who might some day overstep his ability to control the situations which his biting, personality had caused.

Still, there was the chance that guy knew where he might get a drink or if it were possible. He needed one, and good.

"Come along, mister!" Williams ordered, motioning him toward, the staircase at the end of the huge hallway "I'll show you around!"

Just then the redheaded sexpot walked up to them.

"Hi, there!" she greeted, smiling at Norton.

"Push off, Mable." Williams ordered.

"I wasn't talking to you!" she snapped, turning and looking nastily at the small man.

"Brush it off!"

She ignored Williams, looking at Norton instead.

Her hand reached out for his arm.

"Might come along with you—if you're interested," she told him, squeezing his arm.

"Shove off—tramp" Williams demanded, pushing her away from Norton,

"Hey, leave the girl alone!"

"You keep out of this—it's none of your damned business!"

Mable smiled helplessly.

"I'll see you later," she told him, looking pointedly at his body. "I think you're cute! Real hot cute, that is!"

She walked away.

When they were alone, Williams turned to him. "Touch her and you might get into big trouble."

Norton just shrugged. One thing he knew, if she offered herself to him, he'd take the chance—it would be well worth it. Getting between her legs, letting her capture all of him in that nice, compact body was too much of a delicious idea. And every action she had directed towards him was an open invitation.

Somehow he knew that she would be around to continue her direct play to get him into bed.

An anxious throb of excitement stabbed through him just at the thought of getting a bed tumble with that broad. She gave him an erection. Shaking his

26

head he tried to think about other things—but it was hard—damned hard.

He followed Williams through the huge house, and one thought seemed to keep returning. *When would Mable be turning up next?*

He hoped soon. Damned soon. He knew it would be sometime today or tonight. She was a broad with hot firecrackers! He could hardly wait to relieve her anguish; and his own building excitement at the idea of their joining in a savage, hot mating.

BODIES 4 SALE, BY CHARLES NUETZEL

Y THREE Y

And the night before, when Jamie Norton was in Mexico with the little tramp, another man was starting on a path that would soon cross his.

George Kayne's fingers moved across the keyboard of white and black, causing the jumping dullness of "Roll Out the Barrel" to bounce through the smoke-filled air of the cheap saloon, whose name he had already forgotten in the medley of other cheap places so much like this one.

Smoke—Drinks. Drunks. And—"Hey, my girl here's got a voice," and a dollar bill drops on the piano in front of him. "How about letting her sing?"

"What'll it be, Miss?" He'd let anybody sing a song or even dance for a bill...

"I'm In the Mood for Love."

Didn't they know anything else? She's slightly drunk, but pretty enough; and from the expression on his face, nobody would ever know about the hurt deep down inside, or the slightly sickened feeling he would get as she slurred over the fact that she didn't know what key she was about to sing in.

That was all part of the act. A frozen smile, and "what'll it be, Miss?"

But this night was different. He was waiting for his agent, Manny Anson. Maybe this would be the night he would get out of this dive and all the dives like this one in which he seemed to be spending his career.

Frankie, the cocktail waitress, stepped up to the piano bar. "This drink just came from the man at the end of the bar—wants to hear 'Down by the Old Mill Stream', sorry about that!" she said, smiling and placing a beer within easy reach.

Frankie was all right. She was sexy as hell and it took one hell of a lot out of him just watching her and her bouncing bosom. She was the kind of woman you couldn't help thinking would be one hell of a swinger in bed. But there was something other than just animal appeal about Frankie. There was something that made him not only want her in bed, but also protect her. She made this dive different from the rest of the dives he had been working in ever since Jamie Norton hit the bottom and he had to make a go at it alone. Most of the girls working as cocktail waitress looked cheap—like whores. Frankie had a sad look about her—a helpless lonely expression in her brown eyes.

She was also different because she seemed to like him. The way she would glance out of the corner of her eye at George. Her shy smile. Most girls didn't go for his kind of guy. Too small. Too quiet. But even though he and Frankie had said very little to each other, there seemed to be awareness and a silent communication between them. He just somehow knew she was interested.

She was lonely, too, he guessed. Maybe he'd ask her out after work tonight it. Especially if the audition went well. Then he would feel like celebrating.

This was a hell of a place to have an audition.

"Mister—play 'Sweet Adeline'—play it for me soft and sweet!" an overly painted, worn-out face asked.

"Sure, anything you want!"

Where was Manny? What the hell was keeping the guy?

"How about letting the lady sing another song?" A second bill fluttered its way toward the small glass which was already half full.

Good tips tonight!

"Sure thing—right after this lady's request..."

He wondered if the blonde would know her key. She didn't. The voice went flat several times and he had to fake the chording to keep her from sounding bad. But he was good at that; he was an ideal pro at playing for amateur singers who had to get half loaded before they had the courage to let the world hear their golden attempts to keep on key. Everybody thought they could sing. Even the good ones numbered in the thousands.

He tried to remember how long ago it was when he'd gone to his first piano bar to solo for the first time before a bored, noisy crowd. He really couldn't remember anymore.

Frankie looked in his direction. That lonely wide-eyed wounded doe expression. She had pretty brown eyes and one hell of a bobbing body. Last night he'd almost gotten around to asking her out, but he'd been side-tracked by a customer, and it was quitting time and Frankie had gone before he got another chance.

He wished to hell that Manny would get over here!

He was just like a kid on his first audition. Maybe because it was so important to him. Maybe because he knew that if he failed this time he would be finished—never given another chance at the vocal bit. And he'd have to return to his one room apartment with its dim lights and dark, old-fashioned furniture from the 1890's and grease-smeared walls. And he'd not be able to face the truth that he really didn't have quite a good enough voice, and that he didn't have quite good enough looks, and that he didn't have quite a good enough personality.

Then he would drink away the smell and taste of defeat. Lonely and beaten like all the other times.

Things weren't like they had been when Jamie Norton was on top. Jamie had seen that his friend, George Kayne, was taken care of with a good job and a good chance to get ahead. It hadn't been only one-way, though. The two of them had worked well together. Norton never had been able to find a better team partner for him. But since Norton had been black-listed by Manny, things hadn't been going so well for Kayne.

A harsh voice cracked: "Okay, move outta the way, Miss...sorry! Gotta get to Georgie boy here. Business. Business."

"So, who do ya think you are, buster?"

"Business, business!"

Manny.

"Hey, Manny, what took you so long?"

Out of the side of Manny's mouth: "Keep it easy—had to build you up real big and then spice things up a bit with an offer of free booze." A beefy hand reached for the tip money on the top of the piano. "This'll probably take care of it..."

Sure, let George pay for everything. Show business! Why'd he get into it? Admit it! Nothing else he could do. Music had been his life; playing piano was something he'd done since his pre-teens.

"What you gonna sing, Georgie boy?"

"Same old thing."

Just then a large man came up. The expression on his ruddy features and slightly glassy eyes was enough to tell George that the man wasn't in any condition to judge anything—or even care about judging anything!

"Mr. Delcado, this is the fellow I've been talking to you about..."

"Okay, okay! Glad to meet you sonny!" That large hand gripped his and for a moment he could almost believe that Mister Big was really interested.

Frozen smiles and glad hands.

That was the trademark of the business world; but it was the very heart and core of the false reality of show business. Smile when you're crying. Pat them on the back when you want to slug their damn teeth down their throats. Everybody loves everybody else!

"You're agent has been talking you up real big," Mr. Delcado said mechanically, hardly noticing whom he was talking to. He and Manny turned and stepped back through the crowd, disappearing into the Mardi Gras of drunken faces and dim smoky atmosphere that hung over the place like a drapery of misty fog.

George reached for the mike. "Ladies and gents, the club is offering a special low spot in the show, tonight..." He wanted to say that this was so very important; and wouldn't they please, pay attention. But. "Normally, guys like me are only allowed to make with the keyboard stuff, but tonight I'm going to give out with a little of the voice."

A scattered applause.

Maybe three or four people had heard him and made a half-hearted attempt to be polite. They turned back to their conversations.

Frankie eyes looked his way and her lips smiled encouragement. He could really go for her this evening. A real swinger. What rolling hips, delightful, fully-stacked breasts. Maybe after the...

Suddenly he felt the old hates and frustrations and years of disgust and heartache rush through him. What did it matter to any of these bastards that he was about to sing his guts out so that maybe some rotten slob who owned a night club would give him a chance to get a new start?

As he started singing, a couple of the people turned his way. The soft words and flow of his voice carried across the darkened room and more people turned. They nudged each other and shushed each other. The noise slowly faded to a quietness that seemed almost tomb-like.

With a great sense of power, he went into his second number.

They liked him all right. Never had he had such a crowd like this before. A bunch of drunks and lonely pick-ups and tramps and men on the make. He had them all clutched in the swell of his voice. It was a wonderful feeling of power. They sighed when he sighed, and cried when he cried.

For his third number he went into a happy swing tempo and the people were tapping their feet and smiling and laughing. The applause afterwards was first only a rippling and then it slowly swelled. After a short moment it was over.

Frankie rushed up through the crowd.

"That was wonderful!" she whispered, her face beaming and her eyes shining with excitement.

Manny pushed toward, them. "Great! Have to rush off right now. Call me in the morning!"

"How'd Mr. Delcado like it?"

"Fine! Said he'd see what he could do. Maybe a spot in—well, call me, tomorrow. Have to rush off!"

He was gone.

George looked silently at the cocktail waitress. "Well, Frankie—whatever that meant; I guess it was something good!"

For a moment he paused, not knowing how to ask the question he wanted to ask, or if he should. Looking into her eager eyes he saw the longing there.

"How about celebrating with me tonight after work?"

She nodded anxiously, then she was called away before they could say anything more.

But it didn't matter now. She had said yes with her eyes and her actions. She'd be waiting for him before she left work. It was funny how lonely people could say so much without many words communicated to each other.

"Say, mister, how about playing 'Down by the Old Mill Stream'?"

Watching Frankie, he didn't mind so much now. As he followed her progress from one table to another, he couldn't help noticing the difference in her movements; they seemed more alive. Happy. Excited.

He could hardly wait to get her into bed caress her full breasts. Feel her naked body squirming against his. That idea sent excited energy and anxious excitement through his whole body.

"Say, you sure sounded good. I mean the singing. Could you do 'My Funny Valentine' for me and my girl?" A dollar fluttered like an autumn leaf into the glass. He hardly noticed.

Nothing was too important right then, except that after work things were going to being different. A little less lonely.

First, there would be drinks; then celebrating with Frankie. Tomorrow would possibly start a new existence for him.

But he didn't really care—right then, anyway—about anything except Frankie.

After work they talked a little. The bartender had brought them drinks. And then later at her place they had, continued the talking and drinking.

He'd learned things about Frankie. Some of the things about the loneliness which her eyes expressed every time they made contact with his.

She'd come to California when she was eighteen. Gone to college. Met a man who said either she'd let him climb into bed with her or she didn't really love him. The affair had been short, but it had broken her in to the sexual side of life.

Then things had worked out pretty fast. They had been drinking for a couple of hours by then and the buzzing effects of the booze worked their passions into a burning pain inside them. They had been sitting on the sofa for a long time, his arm around her body, her hand touching his leg and thigh. She was warm and affectionate.

He was finding it continually more difficult to keep from taking her in his arms. The position was just right, and her full red lips were only inches from his.

Both held their breath for a long moment. Then suddenly she pulled away and stood.

"I'll be right back," she smiled warmly, leaning over towards him and pressing her lips on his. It was one of those closed mouth caresses that sent a man out of his head. He wanted to pull her into his arms right then.

She moved away and then a moment later she disappeared into her bedroom.

He took out a cigarette from his jacket pocket and lit it. Nervously he puffed on it, blowing smoke into the air. The very thought of what she must be doing was enough to make him feel shaky inside. It was as if he was being pulled into a whirlpool of ecstatic excitement and the suspense was overwhelming.

He reached for his drink and downed it in one gulp. One thing he could say for Frankie, she was one hell of a woman; and that was for damn sure! The bedroom door opened and Frankie stood there.

He swallowed hard, finding it difficult to catch his breath. She was just about the most beautiful, sexy thing he had ever seen. The lacy negligee, which was loosely draped around her body, hardly did anything to hide the fact that she had a terrific body. Every curve showed through the thin netting. He found it hard to keep his eyes away from the full, supple swells of her breasts, which peeked through like curiously waiting eyes.

She slid across the room towards him, her eyes sparkling and the corners of her lips turned upwards in a happy anxious smile.

"Hello there, baby!" he sighed. He reached up and pulled Frankie down to him. She came willingly and hungrily into his arms, her lips parted and trembled slightly under his.

The kiss lasted long enough to get them both stretched out full length on the sofa and then slowly he pulled aside the lacy netting and started exploring every curve and swell of her body. It was sheer delight—the feel of her silky, velvet flesh was like smooth cream. He couldn't keep his eyes off her— or his eager hands. Her response was remarkably, swift and passionate. She seemed to have been hungrily waiting to be made love to for some time, for now that they were close and kissing and caressing, she squirmed and writhed in pleasant agony. Her breathing was heavy and intense; Her whole body became a sea of quivering, excited flesh, that lurched with every touch as if given an electric shock.

It seemed as if all the energy in his body was being sucked out of him as they clutched tightly to one another. Her lips once more made contact with his. Her tongue was a delicious darting target, moving with his with a hunger all its own.

He moved his hand down to her breasts, slowly stroking and fondling them, excited by her frenzied response of her body as it moved under his.

Then they couldn't stop. The anxious beating of her heart as it pounded against his searching and caressing fingers began to match the desperate agony in his own chest. The flood of passion became too heated, too stimulating and overwhelming as they churned frantically and desperately against one another until their fiery explosive need had been burned out of them.

Afterwards the need was still powerful in them.

He had known women in the past; but never one that affected him like Frankie. They rested, and then he felt her move once more.

Her body pressed up against his, and he felt the excited fullness of her—as she breathed heavily. Her hands clawed at his back with an almost painful intensity. The need and electric power of that one embrace left them both weak and—breathing heavily in each other's arms. They tried to relax, but found it impossible. They looked at each other for a long time in silence. Only the soft, drifting sound of music filled the air.

Again they kissed, slowly embracing each other with lips, arms and body. They didn't stop until the ocean of desire had been silenced and their needs and passions soothed once more.

BODIES 4 SALE, BY CHARLES NUETZEL

⟡ **FOUR** ⟡

The next day George Kayne waited in the outer room of Manny Anson's Beverly Hills Office, remembering. He had been waiting for almost twenty minutes to get in to see his agent. It didn't bother him today as much as it might have the day before. Nothing could bother him today—not after last night with Frankie and her passionate body.

It was funny how just one evening with the right girl could change a man's life so much. It was more than sex—though he had to admit that the physical side was pretty wild. He felt different than he had in years. Relaxed and almost happy—at ease with the world—even in Manny Anson's reception room. It was silly. Just one evening with a broad who knew how to make with the hot sex bit—and he was all falling to bits.

But they had seemed to fit—more than just sexually. And that had been pretty wild.

The delight of the following hours of making love to Frankie, who felt all the lonely aches which he felt, had been wonderful.

"Mr. Anson will see you now!"

The words came from far away. At first he didn't recognize who it was or from where it came; or what it said. It was floating on an ocean of black,

41

coming out of the night, from nowhere.

He returned slowly to the world of reality The dream world of memory slid away, replaced by the clean white office of Manny Anson's reception room.

His eyes turned towards the secretary. Her expression was impersonal, but smiling. The business smile of a woman was learned in the art of looking pleasant but also stone-faced. Her job was to let those people in who had business; but also to turn down those whom Manny didn't wish to see. She smiled now, because that was her job.

"Mr. Anson will see you now," she said once more.

He stood. Collected his thoughts, nerves, and emotions to meet what lay behind that closed door.

* * * * * * *

Two hours later Manny Anson was at Mr. Delcado's mansion, being ushered into the man's private office.

The quick conversation between the two men came directly to the point. Delcado sat in his over-stuffed chair—Manny, in the rigid and uncomfortable one.

"You got the piano-man for the deal?"

"Yes, boss!"

"Well, I got Norton. He's in."

Delcado leaned forward and looked carefully at the smaller man sitting so stiffly before him. "This Kayne fellow. He doesn't know that Norton's connected with the deal?"

"No sir! I just told him about the job for tonight. He thinks that it's only a gig!"

"Good."

"But I said there's a possible contract for a club spot—and all he had to do was try out here. Said that Mr. Delcado wanted to see how he worked in a party. You know—the things you told me to say."

"Good. Good! With the party tonight things should work out just as planned. And from then on the next steps should be easy. With each one of them in on this deal, they won't be so quick to question the business going on around them."

After that, Manny left the room. He was taken to his private quarters at the Delcado mansion. Quarters which he was in the habit of using at least once a week. From here at the Delcado mansion and the party coming on this evening, he'd get all the hot willing sluts he might want. To hell with Esther no-name!

This, at least, softened the ego-blow that bitch last night had caused. A nowhere, desperate, starlet trying to get ahead in the show-biz game and then having the gall to turn him down when he tried to make her a deal.

Sleep with me, baby, and I'll make you famous!

She wasn't smart enough to know what a nasty little lie that was. Cheap promises for a hot session with a woman's body.

Bitch! Little slut! He thought angrily, remembering how the woman had simply said no way!

A million like her who were more than willing to spread the goodies to a guy like him.

Screw her! Nothing important!

Sure. But it rankled him. If he saw Esther what's-her-name again he'd make sure she didn't get to first base. Not with anybody! He'd screw her in ways she couldn't even guess at and make the bitch wish she'd screwed him silly last night!

* * * * * * *

Esther Vivian angrily started her car and pulled it out into traffic. She couldn't help feeling a deep inner confusion. Damned Manny Anson! Still, it was a mess. In one way she was glad that things had worked out like they had. It gave her time to think things out a little better.

It was one thing to give a man your body for the price of a possible screen test or a possible club appearance or a possible television appearance, but it was something that had to be handled with care and planning. She wasn't a cheap tramp. And not about to become a couch toy. But that's where she was heading. Right into some SOB's clutches. Unless she found a way out. And that was her own fault— she didn't plan things out very carefully. Just jump first and then think later—but that wasn't so smart.

The night before, when they had been with Manny Anson, and the man had suggested that they go on up to the apartment, she'd acted like a fool.

He'd just moved his arm around her. They were waiting for the traffic light to change and he was taking a chance making a direct and blunt offer to her.

"We might have a little fun," he told her, squeezing her shoulder and pushing his thin lips against her cheek. It took every bit of will power she had had to keep from shivering visibly.

Then she'd exploded. "I think you had better take me home!"

It had been a damn fool thing for her to do, she realized in the morning; but then, it was too late.

Anson had been her first big chance to get in good with an important person. Manny Anson, sharp promoter and agent, a man who could make and break stars.

She'd been told: *Look what he'd done for Jamie Norton several years ago!*

So that morning she'd tried to get a hold of him, but he wasn't in at his office—not for her, anyway.

Then she'd gone to his apartment. But he wasn't there, either. So she waited.

Now she felt that maybe the earlier determination and change in her attitude about the moral rights and wrongs of selling her body for a possible chance to get ahead hadn't been so smart after all. She'd wanted to get hold of Manny and climb into bed with him. If that was necessary. Well he hadn't been around to be had. But the frustrations were again beginning to confuse her. Give in to some producer or agent who wanted to take her to bed on the small chance that they might also be able to help her get a start in show business. Once more she was beginning to wonder.

It was that old trap: you played the game or you were out of the game! Flat on your back in the gutter or flat on your back in some slob's bed.

Some choice!

Parking her car in the garage, she stepped out, walked up to her apartment and opened the door.

"You there, Ruthie?" she called, stepping across the small room toward the kitchen.

"Yes, in here," came a voice from the bathroom. "Taking a shower."

She needed a drink to relax her tired and grated nerves; something to numb her jangled nerves. She had to stop thinking so much!

Quickly pouring a drink, she sat down, at the breakfast table, looking, out across the room at the modern paintings, which her roommate had done several months before and hung up.

Carefully she sipped her drink, letting the golden liquid slowly slide down her throat. It was gently relaxing and good tasting and just what she needed to help her think with less pain, emotion and tension.

Think about what she wanted to become. Be a starlet and maybe some day a star: a famous Hollywood star whom everybody would read about in the movie magazines. The talk of the nation. A person that all the young girls in small and large towns across the country would look up to and want to be like—not realizing the price which had to be paid in pride and self respect.

Famous. Or unknown?

She was back to that again.

Ruth stepped out into the living room then, pulling a blue robe around her slender, nude figure. Ruth was a good-looking woman, Esther realized. How many men had the woman been forced to sleep with to get where she now was? And where was that, really? Just a few movie and TV parts—a couple of minor plays—just a start! For the price of how many searching hands and hungry lips? A few parts for a good-looking girl with talent to boot, Ruthie was still just another struggling starlet! Among the countless others who had come before her and would be there after she had been long forgotten.

"What happened to you, Esther?" The girl asked, looking inquisitively at her roommate. "Forget? Did you forget?"

"Forget what?"

"The party. The party, tonight!"

"Oh, no!" Esther cried in alarm, "Another party? I just can't! Not tonight!"

"But this one's big! You gotta go!" Ruth insisted, pulling her robe tighter around her slim body,

"What do you mean, I gotta go?" She felt an irritation come over her. She didn't have to go any place, if she didn't want to.

"There'll be a lot of people there. The Hollywood crowd. I had one hell of a time getting an invite for you; you can't let me down now." Ruth looked hard at her and then frowned. "Something wrong?"

"No, not really!" She didn't want to talk about it. Not even to Ruth. Least of all to Ruth.

"Then, come on, start getting ready. We only have an hour or so."

She thought it over.

Briskly, but carefully. *Ruth,* she now realized, *must have gone to some trouble to get the invitation to the party for her.*

The girl was trying to help. She was doing the best she knew how to give Esther a chance, and it would be a downright rotten trick to turn her down. It really would not be right to back out now. Anyway, there was always tomorrow to think about problems. A party meant free food and drinks—and that would be good for her. Maybe a very good idea; it would be much better than sitting around all, by

47

herself. People would help, and maybe she would meet somebody else—and then not have to bother with Mr. Manny Anson.

Yes, that was one thought she really liked. "Okay, kiddo! You sold me! To a party we will go!"

FIVE

Norton sat back in the large leather chair, looking up at the ceiling, one hand holding a glass filled with a strong triple shot of whiskey over the rocks.

This was his first real chance to sit, quietly and think about things. Events had happened so fast that he hadn't been able to work them out completely.

Williams had shown him around the huge mansion on a quick cook's tour, which now in his memory was only a blur of rooms, all seeming to blend into each other. Just a series of sizes and shapes without any meaning. It was like being introduced to a group of people. You recognized them, repeated their names, said how glad you were to meet them, and then forgot who they were. The bald-headed man had whipped him through small rooms, big rooms, little big rooms, large small rooms. Told him what they were for. Then the two of them had gone to the room Delcado had assigned to Norton for the evening

And there he found a pleasant surprise. He discovered that his host had set him up with a small bar supply

"He does this for all his new people," Williams explained to him. "And also with most of his old buddies, too! A generous, man."

A generous man, all right. That was a good laugh. A generous man with crooked, dirty money. The guy could afford to be generous with his kind of money.

You should talk, Norton! What kind of money do you think you will be making from now on? That was a good question, he realized. Delcado hadn't mentioned anything about salary. It was assumed, but no figure had really been mentioned. They hadn't even come near the subject, now that he thought about it.

He asked Williams.

"Don't worry none about money. You'll be taken care of. You'll get a private car to use, an expense account, and an office at both clubs; free booze and food facilities. All rights to dip into the till, as long as you don't over-do any of these. Delcado doesn't care how you operate, just as long as there's a big profit involved for himself. And don't forget—it has to be a good profit. You'll also be given some kind of salary, along with an apartment all paid for. The boss likes to keep his boys happy. If they're happy, he doesn't have to worry about them turning against him, and that's the way he likes it!"

After a few friendly drinks of whiskey, the man left. Williams had refused to tell him any more about business after that. "After the party. Tomorrow I take you to the clubs and show you around. It'll be easier that way," had been his parting shot.

For some reason Norton got the idea that the man didn't trust him. Well, that didn't make any, difference, really. He didn't like Williams. Delcado was the boss and that was all that counted! As long as the boss liked him and trusted him, the others could go to hell and back for all he cared.

Then that thought, which had been hounding him for some time, returned: Why had he been chosen? Why had they taken him from a Mexican hellhole, shaken him dry of the dirt and grime and then dipped him into their own kind of filth? From bum to manager of two nightclubs which were to have his name on them.

It didn't really seem to figure completely. Why should they pick him? A has-been. Out of the blue. A finished punk. Hot-tempered. Drunk. Bum. It seemed like they could have gotten along without Jamie Norton on the marquee. There must be plenty of people willing to...

No, maybe there weren't! Maybe it took a guy who had been having a hard time of it—one willing to play ball with a shady deal. Somebody who had hit rock bottom. Gambling was against the law in California. That could be part of it.

He'd no doubt been chosen because he would be in no position to quibble; in fact, willing to jump at any deal. Use his name. People still knew about Jamie Norton. There were still *Jamie Norton* movies playing around. It was just that he couldn't get a job any more. Nobody was willing to take a chance on his hot temper. Manny had had trouble keeping him on the job, even before they broke up, because of his temper and his over-drinking.

Still, they wanted to use his name because people would come to a Club in order to see him; just on the chance of seeing the famous star. It would also draw the Hollywood crowd—fat cats and rich-people. For his name. That was the reason everyone had given him.

Of course, there was Lilly Benton. She, no doubt, was almost entirely responsible for selling him to Delcado. But it was still hard to figure out, for sure. And Manny Anson was part of it all. That was the most troublesome element.

Manny Anson, a person who shouldn't have all that much power—and that he was somehow able to swing it around. Manny Anson could make and break a top star. On careful consideration, it seemed incredible that Manny could have so much power—all by himself.

But, was he alone?

So much power.

It never had seemed logical. Just, a small time agent.

Could it be Delcado? Was he behind Manny? Was he some kind of silent partner, the real power behind the "throne"?

That thought jolted him. He felt his hands begin to tremble and become sweaty. His guts started to turn inside him and he knew his face had started to whiten.

Delcado and Anson. Power brokers?

Could that explain the strong sword that Manny held in his hands? It could!

It could also explain his connection to Delcado—if there was any. After all, it was quite possible that his host had merely called Manny in for entertainment for the party this evening. That might explain it all.

Nothing seemed to figure out right this afternoon. And now, for the first time, it occurred to him that maybe his splitting with Manny hadn't been all that it seemed. At the time it had seemed right enough, but looking back from the viewpoint of this possible new information, it took on another shade of color and meaning.

Now the ideas that were swimming around in his skull were beginning to make him lightly sick. He stood up hastily and walked over to the small liquor cabinet in the corner of the room. He filled his glass with whiskey, then bolted it all down.

The fire helped. It burned at the bottom of his stomach and then bounced dizzily up to his head. That was good! That helped.

His forehead was starting to moisten with sweat. Sluggishly he raised his hand and wiped it dry. It had all happened a long time ago, but the facts still prevailed profusely vivid in his memory:

July 7, 1958. The place: Manny Anson's private apartment. The people: Just Jamie Norton and his agent. Norton was pretty high from having had one too many martinis at the cocktail party given by the press that afternoon.

Manny was talking. "Look here, Jamie. I made you and I can break you!" The man was puffing on a cigar and every once in a while using it to stab at the air—much like Delcado used his finger! "I didn't like what rolled out today!"

It was from left field. No reason. Just explosion number one—as if the man were trying to start a fight.

"What the hell?" Norton managed

to gulp, reacting violently to this sudden attack at his personal behavior. At the time he hadn't realized how unwarranted the series of words were. He had just reacted—not thinking. The drinks had numbed his deeper mental processes and now just animal temper flooded into being.

"And another thing—you better lay off that bottle kick!" There was another silence while he reacted to that statement.

"And I might add, I don't like you running around with that Lilly Benton girl, either!"

That one hit home, but good. "What the hell do you mean? It's none of your damn business who I go out with. And I'll drink as much as I please. You can go to hell!"

The silence had been deafening after that.

They both seemed to be on the verge of murder. A long heated quiet before the thunderous storm.

Manny just stared at him, a queer expression moving across his flushed features. "What's that you just told me to do?" he demanded, the words coming out slowly, and with an accent on each one.

"If you think that you can run my private life, then you can—go—to—hell! And stay there!"

Norton had never been quite as mad as he was then. At the time he and Lilly were having a raging love affair; it was the peak of their mutual attraction for each other—later, several months after he had walked out on Manny, they broke up; the passion burned out, but the friendship was strangely stronger than ever.

That long silence raged again.

"I'll just tell you this once more. When it comes to business, your action in private life will always be edited. And by me! You got that? I'll tell you exactly what to do! You got that clear?" The bottle in his right hand slammed down on the top of the bar, making a loud banging sound.

Biting his lower lip, Norton calmly walked over to the front of the bar and looked deep into Manny's eyes. "Okay, buster, since it's time to complain, I might as well throw my two-bits in!" He swallowed hard, holding down the burning agony of the near madness threatening to take over his muscles and mind. "I think you stink as an agent. I don't like giving you fifty percent of everything I make and I think it's about time you wrote up a new contract— or we're through!"

Manny's face sobered. His lips tighten into a hard knot. "You walk out and Mister Jamie Norton, you are through! Finished! Dead! No more jobs. Nowhere! No more money! Nothing!"

The outburst left both of them slightly dazed and breathless.

"I mean that, Norton!"

"Then you can go to hell!" Norton had yelled, turning and walking out.

The next day he had discovered that his contract had been suddenly cancelled at the studio. No reason given. And his recording contract ended without any explanation. His night club engagements stopped, without warning.

He tried to get another agent but nobody would touch him. He even tried to get hold of Manny, half willing to beg himself back into the man's favor. Anson was out for Jamie Norton, period! It didn't take any mental giant to figure out what had happened. Manny had been true to his word. He was blackballed. No more jobs. Finished. Ended. Nothing!

And that was it. The end of his career.

He and Lilly had taken a trip around the world then and in England he had tried his act at some of the clubs there. It was one big flop. Several other countries were just as uninterested in him.

Lilly had been pretty nice and morally helpful throughout the whole trip, but when they returned to the States their heated passion suddenly faded out. They were just one day out at sea when the lid blew off their relationship. Lilly was in their cabin taking an early nap—but at the time he didn't realize that. All he knew was that he was alone, half drunk and nothing to do. He was on his way out of one of the lounges when he accidentally bumped into a beautiful redhead. There was enough liquor buzzing in his brain for him not to care about anything in particular except the sensual quality of anyone or anything—at that moment, this beautiful woman.

She looked up and smiled brightly.

"Hello! Who are you?" she murmured, leaning closer and letting her arms slip around his neck. She was drunk and the offer was direct and to the point. She wanted to get together with a man—and didn't care really who it was. The way her body moved against him and the nearness of her lips was enough to start him off right then. But even on shipboard it would be making things too fast to suggest that they find some quiet cozy corner. So he had led her to the bar, and ordered a few rounds of drinks.

The conversation was general and meaningless. He didn't even try to remember it. The drinks came and were downed. The world spun around faster and faster. A couple of more rounds and somehow the two of them were walking along the corridor, singing and half leaning on each other. After a slight blackout he found himself in some stateroom. He had forgotten all about Lilly in his drunken fog. It seemed only a few moments later that the woman was nakedly crushing herself to him.

"Hmmm...." she sighed, her lips parting and the invitation of her tongue moistly seeking his. It was only a matter of seconds before they were ready to climb to the peak of sexual ecstasy. She was leaning against the door, and for some reason they didn't even think of going into the bedroom. She squirmed and jerked and wiggled. It was almost impossible to find her because of her wildly thrashing body. But finally they surged together and locked for a long series of throbbing convulsive passion moments.

That's when Lilly Benton stepped out from the bedroom.

There was a scream of insane rage and a moment later he felt himself being ripped from the naked woman. Then he heard more yells of rage and pain.

The fog of his brain tried to clear away, but it was impossible.

Somewhere in that dazed dimension he heard the word "bitch" and "whore" and "slut", but he couldn't—at first—concentrate on what was being said or was happening.

Finally he managed to push back the blanket of mental sluggishness and see what was going on around him.

Lilly and the woman he had brought with him were twisting and clawing, biting and kicking each other on the floor. One moment Lilly was on top and then the next the woman was slugging down at the actress face with a clawed hand. Lilly had on what was left of a pink nightgown; it was now shredded filmy lace.

"Come on, girls!" he yelled, yanking Lilly away from the other woman. "Stop it!"

The power of his voice seemed to attract their attention. There wasn't another word said. The woman he had brought into the stateroom gathered up her clothing, quickly dressed and left.

Lilly didn't say anything about the matter, but she also refused to let him make love to her that evening. That was one thing that he could never forgive a woman. At least not then. Refuse him once and they were finished.

When they reached New York they made up and the session in bed together had been the greatest, but after that they didn't see each other for a long time. It wasn't anybody's fault. Maybe just because he now knew that he was finished as an entertainer; and that Lilly was still on top. He didn't want to be hanging on. It wouldn't have looked good. Anyway, all he knew was that his passionate desire ended with the trip. No regrets. Just good friends when they met. Now it was over. The romance finished.

But, looking back at the whole thing it seemed suddenly unnatural. It didn't figure that so many things could go wrong so quickly.

It was almost as if everything had been planned, mapped out for some unreal reason.

It all seemed, now, as if Manny had deliberately plunged into an argument in order to break things off; as if he had gone out of his way to make Norton explode and walk out. Manny knew about his hot temper and maybe he had used it as a weapon against him. But why? Why kill a good money-maker?

And now, come to think of it, he could see other things that might fit into the puzzle. Too many little things that hadn't seemed to mean anything at all at the time they took place.

He wondered why he hadn't seen it before.

Yet now he grimly wondered exactly what the facts might be. The truth wasn't particularly obvious. Only that there was more than met the eye.

The events and incidents and circumstances were attempting to form into a picture within his mind, but he wasn't quite sure what it looked like, or what it was he should be investigating. He was now searching for the first time—but for what? Somehow he had to get the answer. Find the truth before it was too late.

The answer, he was sure, must be in this Delcado mansion—with his host, Manny Anson, and maybe Lilly Benton, too.

Just then somebody knocked at his door. He

59

snapped upright. The sound startled him.

Then a voice sounded, calling, "Are you there?"

It was a woman's voice.

He walked over to the door and opened it.

Standing there before him was the woman whom he had first met in Delcado's office and then later in the hallway. Williams had called her Mable.

"Hello," she smiled, stepping in before he had a chance to stop her.

The way her hips wiggled and the flashing expression in her flirting eyes was enough to tell Norton exactly why she was here. As if that was necessary. A woman seldom came into a man's room, closing the door behind her, with purely innocent motives. The skin-tight dress, cut low in front, half revealing her milk-white, full breasts was enough to make him more than interested in what she might have planned.

The warning that Williams had given him about her flashed in his mind. But he shook his head as he closed the door, and then turned toward the woman.

One way or another it looked like the afternoon wasn't going to be as uninteresting as he had thought it might.

That was for damn sure!

Mable had more than a pretty body—it was sex all the way. "I thought maybe you might give me a drink," she told Norton, leaning against the small bar cabinet. Her smile was the hottest come-on lie he had ever seen.

"Sure, sure thing," he told her, stepping up beside her and starting to fix her a cocktail. His temples were throbbing with heated excitement. He didn't know what she really had in mind, or if, maybe, Delcado had sent her up here to do a little spying on his new man—and he didn't care one hell of a damn!

"I hear that Del hired you..." she commented conversationally, taking the drink he provided her and then starting to swing her way across the room toward the sofa on the far side. Watching the action of her body was something that almost took his breath away. It was animal sex and nothing else, but it was enough.

"I—I'm taking over the two—"

"Clubs—I know *all* about it!" She patted the sofa next to her. "Come on over and sit..." Her voice trailed off so that all the implication that was possible to get into those words was left dangling electrically in midair.

He somehow found his way over to where she was. The effect of her body and the way it was staged in that low-cut dress, was enough to excite any normal male.

She leaned close to him, her lips only inches from his. "I think you're cute—you know that, so why don't you kiss me?"

With one swift motion she put her drink on the stand next to the sofa and then pulled the top of her dress down so that her large full bloom breasts were nakedly exposed.

"Wouldn't you like to touch and stroke these?" she asked, moving closer to him.

He couldn't believe his eyes. This didn't happen in real life.

"What kind of gag is this?" he demanded. He'd seen fast women before, but this was pushing things much too fast He gulped and drew his eyes away from those lovely, pink-tipped wonders.

"Come on let's have a little fun! I'm hot all over…for what you have…down there!" She looked directly at his crotch. "Looks real juicy to me!"

"I said, what's the gag?" he demanded, standing.

"Del sent me up!"

"That's a lie and you know it!"

Just then the door swung open and Delcado came marching in. His face was red with anger and his fists tight and white. "Okay, you little tramp— get out of here! And now. I see you in your room!"

She didn't say a word. There didn't seem to be any reaction from her at all. Very calmly she stood, replaced her dress and then after reaching for her drink and downing it she slowly walked out.

When she was gone Delcado turned toward Norton. "I'm sorry about this. She's got hot pants for any man who comes along!"

He turned furiously around and then walked out slamming the door behind him.

Norton just stood there frozen with surprised shock and disbelief. One thought was hammering through his mind. That it hadn't been a gag. That the girl was a nympho—and that was okay with him. It was just that before he had been too surprised at her sudden breast display that he hadn't had time to recover or really think about it. Now he knew that she'd made an open, direct offer, and really meant it.

It was just a good thing that he hadn't taken her up on it. There was no telling what Delcado might have done to him.

He walked over to the bar-cabinet and mixed another drink. Downed it and then stepped over to the bed and lay down on his back. He'd need rest for the party. That was for sure. Plenty of rest.

And if he just got one chance to get at Mable again -just one more chance—he could hardly wait, just thinking about it.

* * * * * * *

Williams stepped to the phone and picked up the receiver. "Hello?" he said carefully looking around to make sure that nobody was in the room with him.

"Tonight at the party." Were the only words.

They were enough. Williams knew that sometime that evening he was supposed to kill both Delcado and Jamie Norton. Finish the two men off and step into the big spot...!

♆ SIX ♆

The Big Hollywood Party.

Norton couldn't have cared less. He had made it a point not to show up until around nine. By then things were already moving along pretty nicely. A bunch of drunken broads—whores starlets, sluts. And he couldn't care less, except for the Mable girl. He kept looking for her. She was just about the sexiest thing alive. At least she sure had a pair that didn't want to keep out of his mind's eyes.

His head was in Cloud 9 by the time he had walked halfway across the large ballroom in which the party was being held. Several times a waiter offering a glass of champagne—which he hadn't once refused, had stopped him.

There were too many requirements for a person at a party like this one. Kiss the girls. Hello and pat the boys on the back. Like a guy had once told him:

"Give them the frozen smile and glad hand treatment."

A little guy with a great talent on the piano and not such a bad voice had told him that. It was funny, he hadn't thought about George Kayne for months. Maybe it was the sound of the combo playing in the background. That sounded a lot like George's style. Norton wondered what had, happened to the little guy. They had been old friends and for a long time worked together. George Kayne had been a good musical arranger for the type of act that Norton had put on. You needed a guy who could be depended on to clown at the keyboard. They had worked well together. Maybe that's why he had flopped so badly in England—George hadn't been with him then.

Those had been good days. But he hadn't allowed himself the luxury of thinking about them.

So many things happening so fast—Too fast. But he was determined to find out the connection between Delcado and Anson. Maybe not tonight— but he would do his damnedest to find out as much as possible. First he would have to scout the territory, then maybe later he would discover a lead which would give him the information he needed to piece together a puzzle that suggested so many possible pictures, but gave no real hint as to the actual form.

"Hi there, lover-boy!" a delightfully familiar voice floated out of nothingness, several yards in front of him. It was soft and lilting, but it still could be easily heard over the sounds of the crowd of people who were already beginning to fill the huge ballroom.

He looked up in the direction of the female voice.

"Hi, Lilly!" he greeted, moving toward the tall, dark-haired woman who was already starting in his direction. Her lips were smiling warmly and her face was bright and happy looking. And those eyes, deep green and delightfully excited.

"It's sure nice seeing you here!" she exclaimed, sliding up to him and running her arms around his neck. Her lips were soft and shiny looking. "Darling, I was afraid you'd turn the deal down!"

"Still the beautiful Lilly Benton I saw a couple of weeks ago!" he laughed, affectionately kissing her. "You haven't aged a minute!"

For a moment the old desire returned. "You never seem to change."

"I can't say that about you." She stepped back and shook a finger in his face.

"I've told you once I've told you a thousand times you drink too much!" She laughed then and took hold of his arm. "I have somebody I think you might want to meet!" She pulled him forward. "Come along!"

He couldn't really think of anybody who might interest him enough to walk across the street to see except maybe Mable. Or Lilly. Maybe he could get some of the information he was seeking from Lilly. That thought stopped him.

"Say, Lilly!" he cried, pulling her back toward him, "I want to talk to you."

"Sure, darling. But can't it wait?" She smiled up at him, her eyes dancing, her lips turned up nicely in that delicately amused expression which was so famous on the screen. "I got a big surprise for you!"

"But this can't wait!" he insisted.

"What are you talking about?"

"This!" he replied, pointing to the whole room in such a manner that the action included the whole building and everything surrounding it.

"Why, this is Mr. Delcado's Hollywood estate!" she laughed brightly. "Didn't you know? You can't be that drunk and lost!"

"No! That's not what I'm talking about. I mean

what is this deal that you've gotten me into?"

"I don't get what you are driving at!" The statement was meant to be an attempt to stop him before he got started. She didn't want to talk about it. But he did.

"Look, Lilly, I'm serious. Why did Delcado want me in on this deal? Why me?"

"Oh, that!" She leaned closer to him, her lips nearing his ear. He couldn't help noticing the crevice between her breasts, and it wasn't too difficult to get a physical reaction from the view he was given. Men simply couldn't avoid such a neckline; and women knew exactly how to package their most charming features. That was their business—especially those in show business.

"It's all my fault! I'm the guilty one!" Then she laughed. "I talked him into it!" This remark was followed with a light snicker, and he realized for the first time that she was slightly loaded.

That was Lilly for you. Give her a drink and she was likely to be loaded as hell in twenty minutes if she was in the mood. Which was most always.

He should have known. But that little mistake could be marked off as his own slightly heady feeling. Anyway, this really wasn't the time or place to talk over such matters. It would have been silly of him to make any attempt at all.

"Can we talk later? Are you going to be in town long?"

She thought that over very carefully, her face becoming quite serious.

"I don't see why not!" she cried, laughing once more. Her eyes began to sparkle again. The light bubbling sound breaking over her delicate but full lips made her white throat shake slightly. She had a lovely throat. Lilly, for that matter, was a beautiful woman. He couldn't and never had tried to deny that—even if their physical attraction for each other had dimmed a long time ago, he couldn't forget the delightfully silky, supple feel of her naked breasts and body.

"You know," she finally said, still smiling. "I'm staying here!"

He looked at her with surprise. "How come I didn't find out sooner?"

"Well, I didn't know you were here, either, until a little while ago. It's a big place!"

He could see that this wasn't the time or place to do anything but enjoy himself. Tomorrow would be soon enough to start trying to piece together the true facts: Then he would get together with Lilly and the question-and-answer period would begin in all seriousness.

He smiled, said: "Well, what was that surprise, you wanted to show me?"

"Come along lover-boy, and mother will show you all!"

They started their way through the crowd, moving in the direction of the corner of the room where the combo was playing a light, arrangement of Misty. The style sounded familiar. It once more reminded him of George Kayne's lacey fingering of the keyboard. This man had the gentle touch of George's magical playing. Then they broke through a group of people and got a good view of the small trio of musicians and his breath slammed out of him.

It was George! Good old George Kayne! He

could hardly believe his eyes. It was good to see him again. It would be one hell, of a ball talking over old times.

Suddenly everything seemed to change from gloom to sheer happiness. He was with Lilly and here was George! His two best friends.

* * * * * * *

Party time for Esther had become a run through a huge mansion, greeting a few friends and now this: the bloody man was following her everywhere. In a way the man wasn't a bad looking sort, Esther thought; trying to get herself interested. He had followed her through the Mardi Gras crowd that had already gathered at the party. Everybody that was anybody was at the party A typical Hollywood affair. From wanna-bees to producers. Professionals and amateurs. Men on the make and starlets willing to be made.

This guy was one of those on the make and she wasn't one of the willing starlets, least of all for him! Instinctively she didn't like the man. Nothing personal—just her first reaction. But there was no way of getting rid of him without being rude. He was tall and redheaded with owl-eyes that looked anxiously through horn-rimmed glasses. Plus the man was a little over-bearing and already slightly drunk.

They were now sitting at the long makeshift bar set up for the affair.

"Well, what'll you have?" he asked, as the bartender appeared and stood silently before them.

"A martini," she ordered from the bar-man, determined not to give her new "boyfriend" any chance to do her any favors. She would have enough trouble getting rid of him. And she realized her brush-off better come pretty fast. Before it was too late and she found herself stuck with his cheering personality for the rest of the evening,

"What's the name you go by?" he asked, laying his arm on her bare shoulder, his hand rested almost at her throat.

"I'm Ken." His fingers squeezed lightly at her neck.

"Call me Vi!"

The drinks came and she didn't wait to be ladylike. Taking a quick swallow of the martini, she ordered another one before the bar-man could get away. The drinks were free and she was in the mood to be slightly drunk. And fast. At least pleasantly high enough to laugh off this kind of situation.

"What do you do?" she asked, turning toward Ken. She wasn't really interested but somehow it seemed that some kind of conversation was necessary. Even if she did plan on dropping him at her first chance. That was one thing about these parties: you got to know somebody fast and if you didn't make any real advances it was possible to dump them just as easily; as long as things didn't get too involved.

"Assistant direction!" he replied, taking on a slight air of false importance.

It was a lie. She could see that from the way he threw the statement off without following it up with anything significant.

"Oh, an assistant director!" she corrected him, in mocked surprise. "Now you are exactly the type of person I don't want anything to do with!"

His face blanched and the smile of importance faded.

The second drink came then and she took it in one hand while with the other disengaged his arm from her shoulder.

"I'll see you around, if you're lucky!" she smiled as sweetly as she could, blew him a violent kiss and moved over toward the three-piece combo in the far corner.

She had gotten only halfway there when she bumped right into Manny Anson. There was a long, frozen silence as he gave her the icy stare.

She forced herself to smile, feeling the chill stab through her.

"Oh, Mr. Anson—I feel horrible about last night. I tried to get hold of you all day."

His expression didn't change. He didn't say a thing.

"That was a silly thing I did—I just didn't well—feel well! You know how it is!" She was chattering like a fool, but she found it impossible to stop.

He finally held up a hand. "Listen, baby! It's over! Good-bye!"

He turned and walked off, making her feel like a bigger fool. She didn't even feel mad—just stupid at, first. After that she became mad.

The idea of that bastard, she cursed inwardly, moving toward the combo again. She'd show him that she didn't need his kind of help. *She'd show that no good rotten bastard!*

There was a small group of people surrounding the piano, and one tall man looked familiar at first but she couldn't place the name that fit with the face. Standing beside him was a beautiful woman whom she immediately recognized as Lilly Benton.

That's when she placed the man's face and name! It was Jamie Norton. He'd been out of the limelight for the past couple of years.

Just imagine, Jamie Norton! She thought, breathlessly. He had been quite a heart-throb when she was younger.

And he was the man she'd use to prove to Manny Anson that he wasn't the only person who could help a woman get ahead in show business. She edged closer, standing on the outskirts of the group.

It was hard to contain the thrill of excitement. And that was completely childish because these were just people. Nothing more. Still, Jamie Norton and his one-time leading, lady, Lilly Benton!

Lilly looked almost as beautiful off screen, as on, she thought, sipping at her martini. A little older, but still pretty.

She felt a dig of resentment toward the other woman. The actress was no doubt with Norton and she suddenly realized that she really wanted to meet him. And then get to know him and somehow— maybe somehow she'd find a way to get him to make love to her. That last was fantasy. Outright make-believe. But it was such a lovely thought.

Just the idea of being taken in his arms...But that was silly! He was Lilly's friend. Her chances were just nothing. Yet, all she needed was one little chance.

You're being a silly little teen-age kid fan. Act your age!

She suddenly realized something about herself. She didn't mind going to bed with someone she might like—that could be different.

With Jamie Norton it wouldn't be so hard—in fact, it would be a pleasure.

A real pleasure!

One that would, naturally, never happen. But what a neat little dream-fantasy.

☿ SEVEN ☿

"Good God!" Kayne fairly yelled, jumping to his feet in a springing leap. "Where the hell did you come from, Jamie?"

"Right *from* hell!"

"Thought I was seeing a ghost!"

"George, old boy! You have no idea how good it is to see you. Lilly said that she wanted to show me a surprise. I would never have guessed." Norton slapped him on the back. "What have you been doing? How're you?"

"Fine, fine! Great, in fact!" Kayne grinned helplessly sitting back down at the piano bench. This is my first real break since you flew out of the State!"

"Sorry about that," Norton said.

"That's silly. Don't blame you..." Kayne cued the other musicians and they started into a light swinging arrangement.

Jamie smiled. "That same old piano-man!"

"Not quite. It looks like I'm getting a chance to give out with the vocal chords at this new gig that's been offered to me." The man's fingers moved along the keyboard as if with a consciousness all their own, as he talked. "What you doing in town?"

"Called in on business."

"In the saving of things again?"

"Might say that. Some people want to back me. Rather they want me to front for them. I'll be in charge of a couple of clubs here in town."

He paused for a moment and then a thought occurred to him. "Say, maybe I'll be able to use a new piano man..."

That's when the strikingly, beautiful blonde stepped up and without any warning whatsoever dumped her drink over the front of Norton's shirt and jacket.

At first he didn't know quite what to do. There seemed to be a long silence. Everybody was paralyzed. His first shocked reaction was not directed at the girl as much as it was on the drink. After the mental surprise came the thought that good liquor had just been wasted on an uncaring shirt and jacket. Then his eyes turned toward the person who had caused the accident. At first he felt anger, then his insides started turning delightful flips. It was as if he'd been whacked hard in the gut, but in a surprisingly pleasant, joyful way.

From anger to wonderment. Women didn't normally affect him like this. They usually didn't have any influence on him except on a purely sexual level. Like Mable. This was different. This wasn't a normal woman—she was something from heaven. Beautiful wasn't the right word for her. Perfection didn't really fit. She would never really win Miss Universe because her features were different from those considered by the judges at such affairs. Yet, she was just about the most perfectly beautiful woman he had ever seen—and he had seen plenty. There was something even more enchanting about her, but he didn't know what. Something in the way her eyes made contact with his. The inner communication which they seemed to be exchanging, silently, with their eyes. Hers were deep blue and lovely. Large and wide looking. They seemed to truly be the doorway to her soul. He was sure they must be.

Never had he seen such beautiful eyes, such honest emotion expressed so openly.

Her lips. Full, but not too large. The lower lip almost pouting—a soft cushion. Her face was almost oval, with high cheekbones. Blonde hair carefully floating around it.

He had always thought that some day he might look up and suddenly see such a vision as this. The girl would be the one of his dreams. One look was all that he would need. Not love at first sight, but that feeling would slowly develop. Love would come as quickly as the sun following morning light on the horizon.

He knew it was silly as hell. But in that first fleeting instant when their eyes made contact he knew the truth. The woman was going to become entangled in his life in some very important way.

"Hell," he whispered, forgetting all about the accident, forgetting about Lilly or Kayne or anything or anybody except this lovely blonde.

"Oh, I'm so sorry!" she exclaimed, her voice high and desperate sounding. The worried expression on her face seemed to make it even more lovely than otherwise. She didn't look like the normal starlet. Not that many of them were deceptively innocent looking. But she had an "untouched" look about her. A woman who had no doubt known the score for some time, yet who hadn't lost that fresh, cleaner side over nature. No matter what the world brought, some soul remained pure.

"Oh...I'm terribly *sorry!*" she cried again.

"Sorry?" At first he didn't realize what she was talking about. Then he remembered his wet suit. "Oh, that's quite all right. You didn't do it on purpose."

Lilly looked helplessly around the room for a moment. "What the hell can we do?"

"Look, I can take care of myself." Norton laughed, feeling rather foolish and not knowing why. "I'll run up to my room and change. Be back in a moment."

"Oh, I'm really so sorry about this. I didn't mean to, really!"

"Forget it!"

"Isn't there anything I can do?"

Lilly turned on the other woman. "Just stop acting so foolish!"

"Lilly!" Norton snapped, trying to soothe her down a bit. She had a bad temper when she let it go. "The girl didn't --"

"I know! She didn't mean to do it!" Lilly snapped angrily, turning and walking away from them.

Kayne laughed, "That's Lil for you!"

Norton didn't get it. There seemed to be no reason for Lilly to have blown up like she had,

"I'm really sorry. Can't I do something?"

"Yes there is. Be here when I get back. You can have a drink with me!"

She laughed at that.

That stopped him short. His eyes caressed over her as if in literal contact.

"I think," she observed, "I already have had a drink…on you."

"Have another," he invited with a quick smile. "But…please…we can leave the suit alone, this time around."

He turned and started across the room.

He couldn't help wonder why Lilly had stormed away. But that was Lilly. All during their love affair there had always been that temper. Maybe that was why they got along so well. They both had good down-to-earth tempers.

He had just closed the door to his room when he saw a shadowy form lying on his bed. Quickly he leaped forward, reaching for the dark, alien figure.

"Who the hell?" he cried in surprise as his fingers dug into a softly familiar breast.

"Hi there, lover-boy!" Lilly's velvet voice murmured in his ear.

He tried to move away but her arms were already around him, hugging him tightly to her naked body.

"What the hell?" he cursed, struggling to get loose from her grip without hurting her.

"Come on, be nice to me!" she demanded, squirming against him.

"Come on—love little old Lilly!" she invited, nibbling his ear lobe. Her breasts were pressing and wiggling on his chest.

"Goddamn you!" he yelled, yanking away and standing. It took only a few moments to get changed. Lilly didn't say anything, but he could feel her eyes fiery with fury, burning into his back.

He left her in the room on the bed. Walking into the big ballroom he returned to where Kayne and his trio were creating mellow musical sounds.

She wasn't there!

"What happened to the blonde cutie?" he asked Kayne, feeling a dizzy cold fear run across his stomach and spine.

"Don't know. She went off the moment you disappeared." Kayne looked up at him, his eyes concerned and serious. "You know she spilled the drink on purpose, don't you?"

"Naturally!" He had to find her but he didn't really know quite why. She was somewhere in the crowd. She had to be. And he was determined to find her.

He wanted to learn about her—her name. Find out where she lived. Make a date. Take her home this very evening if possible.

At least he wanted to get her phone number. But before he could do that he would have to find her.

That's when he noticed her across the room. She was sitting at the bar talking to a man. But that didn't stop him.

* * * * * * *

Esther hadn't at first known quite what to do. All she knew was that she wanted to somehow get to meet Norton. Then without even thinking she had walked up and spilled her drink on him.

The plan of action—what little there had been— fell apart after that. All she was aware of was what a silly thing she had done. How would that get her into the good graces of a total stranger?

Then their eyes had met and confusion welled up in her. A magic moment seemed to flutter over

80

them, stopping the forward movement of time. In that long instant a lot of things seemed to happen. Then they were shattered by Lilly Benton's sharp voice.

Everything happened fast after that.

She tried to make him understand that she hadn't meant it, but felt that all that she did was botch the whole thing. Every word seemed to get her in deeper. They sounded less believable. Then Lilly blew up and she realized that the other woman had seen through the awkward attempt that she had made to get attention. Her first thought after that was to wonder if Jamie Norton had realized the truth. But he didn't seem to.

Then the invitation for her to stay around until he got back. At first she was going to do just that, then sudden shame and confusion took over. All she wanted to do was escape. She walked away the moment Norton had disappeared. First she needed a drink. She needed to think things over. She felt like a damned fool! And totally knocked off-balance by the almost soul shattering silent communication that had jolted her when their eyes had met.

The trouble with her was that she didn't reason things out before she did them. She wanted to meet Jamie Norton. So what does she do?—Spills her drink over him. That was a brilliant way to make friends. Smart!

Finally she made her way through the crowd and to the bar.

"Give me a martini," she ordered as the barman stepped up to her.

"Hi, baby," a voice cried out from behind her. She felt a heavy hand fall on her shoulder and squeeze, as of conveying some secret signal. "Came back to your old lover-boy, after all, did you?"

She turned in surprise. It was the redheaded Ken. Just the person she didn't want to see right now.

Ken sat down beside her. "I thought you'd come around again."

"Oh?" She turned and looked coldly at him, making her voice seem like something from the far north.

"What's with you, baby?"

"Nothing. Just exactly nothing!" she smiled icily. "Just that I don't like men!"

He laughed at that and patted her thigh and before she could reach down and pull his hand away. "You're a real jolt! A girl like you not liking men. That's like saying a fish doesn't like water. Birds don't fly."

The drink came and she gulped half of it down before she realized what she was doing.

They sat in silence for a long time, and for this she was glad. There didn't seem to be any nice way of discouraging him. All he had to do was make one more pass and he'd find an open palm in his face. Hard across his face.

She sipped her drink. Ate the olive and ordered another martini.

"Baby, you sure are drinking it down!"

"That's none of your business."

"Sorry."

She didn't hear the rest of what he said. She wasn't listening. Instead, her brain just mentally blocked out all sound.

She felt a hand touching her thigh. That was the

first moment she realized that she'd made a mistake not paying any attention to the man's conversation. Then a soft voice whispered in her ear.

"Why don't you and I ditch this party? I know of a certain place…"

She felt fingers searching in a very nervous manner along her leg and that's when the explosion took place. One swing was all that was needed. Her hand slapped across his face so hard that the sound seemed like the snapping of a huge wooden beam.

The shocked expression on his face turned abruptly to a distorted rage.

"You little whoring bitch!" he cried, doubling up his fist and starting to swing it in her direction.

BODIES 4 SALE, BY CHARLES NUETZEL

♈ **EIGHT** ♈

Norton saw it all from the beginning when the young man drunkenly leaned toward Esther, placing his hand on her thigh, until she turned and gave him the hardest slap that he had ever seen a woman lay across the face of a man.

A quick mental note impressed itself on his mind not to ever get this lady mad at him.

By that time he was almost up to them. At first he wasn't quite sure what he should do since this matter wasn't really any of his business. Then the fist went back ready to whip forward.

He didn't stop to think or hesitate.

It took only two actions on his part. One hand reached out toward the other man turning him around to meet another doubled up fist.

The swing was perfect, the timing right. The connection exactly on target. Right on the point of the man's jaw. The lights had no doubt gone out the moment his fist had struck. The man fell to the floor, his arms and legs shooting out in all directions.

"Let's get out of here." Norton cried, turning and taking hold of Esther's arm.

In minutes they were outside. Then he realized that there really wasn't any place to go.

85

"You okay?" he asked, looking at her.

"I think so." Her voice sounded shaken.

They stood looking at each other and saying nothing for a long while. There didn't seem anything to say for a moment.

Then finally he suggested, "Want to take a ride somewhere?"

"That's what I slapped Ken for suggesting!" she laughed almost in delight. "God, that little creep tried to not only hit on me, but actually hit me!" Her voice shook with emotion with those last words.

"Well, that's that!" Norton exploded suddenly. "No car!"

"I got one," she smiled, taking his hand and squeezing it gently. It was a soft, lovely, ever so gentle seductive invitation. "Ruthie will find someone to take her home. She usually does—if she comes home tonight at all, that is."

She directed them to where her car was parked, gave him the keys and a little later they were on their way out of the Delcado estate.

"By the way, my name's Jamie—and what's yours?" he asked, turning to look at her for a moment.

She laughed nervously and then said: "Esther."

Out of the corner of his eye he watched her light a cigarette and drag deeply on it. She then leaned back; resting her head on the leather covered seat. Her breathing was light and she seemed quite naturally relaxed, as if this were the most normal course of events.

Yet somehow he knew that she wasn't the type of girl to let herself be picked up. There was more class sitting next to him than he'd known for years.

He was driving slowly, almost thoughtfully and the time it took them to get off the Delcado estate and onto the main highway seemed much longer than the actual five minutes. He unconsciously headed the car in the direction of the beach.

"I'm sorry about the spilled drink," she said in a low whisper.

"That's all right."

"I—I don't know why...really so rude of me! I did it on purpose!"

The words seemed to pop out of her mouth as if she had been forced to push them out against her will.

"I know," he told her.

"What?"

He laughed. "Nobody could have been so awkward as you were. It was too obvious. The expression in your eyes gave you away."

She joined him in the laughter and from that moment on they were good friends.

Just like that!

"I am sorry."

"Don't be. But what I'd like to know is—why'd you do it?"

"Well, it isn't every day that a girl like me gets a chance to meet Jamie Norton," she replied, half seriously.

"Why? Why bother?"

Silence answered the question. He guessed the rest. *A girl who wanted to have a chance to get ahead in show business would do many things for that first break—even trying to ...*

He didn't like the finish of that thought for two reasons. One, because he didn't like to think of

Esther as being that kind of a woman; and for the other reason, that was something personal—no man liked to think a woman would let him take her to bed just to get some crappy favor.

At least he didn't like the idea.

Well. Not with Esther, anyway.

A whore was something else: that was a case of taking advantage of the woman—not the other way around.

"How long have you been in Hollywood?" he asked, not looking in her direction. He didn't want to see her as she answered the next few questions. He wanted the answers but he didn't want to see the expression on her face as she gave them.

And that was pretty childish of him. He had picked up this broad just like he might have some cheap starlet or tramp or whore. Sure, he had to admit to himself—he'd like to climb into bed with her. Like instantly. But that hadn't been his motive this time. Well, at least, not his prime reason.

"How long in Hollywood?" she repeated in a lost-sounding, soft voice. "I really hardly know. Maybe six months, and then maybe six years. Just this day has seemed like six years. It all seems like forever when I think of the struggles and difficulties."

Her voice had faded into silence and he let it lie there for a long moment.

"I think I know what you mean," he heard himself say. "Time seems to stand still for some people—at certain times. And you look out and watch things happen. You experience life. Maybe cry or laugh, and you're happy or sad. But time slows down for you. It makes things seem more important and stand out against the blackness of the rest of your life. Everything becomes an endless drape of grayness against the few splotches of bright color when time is brought to a stop."

A long silence settled down over them. It was melodramatic. That's when he began laughing again. He felt, more than heard, her laughing in the seat next to him. "I've never been quite so corny in my life before."

She laughed a light, throaty bubbling sound. "It was—well put. I loved it!"

They both laughed at that.

"Odd," he remarked, "how a person will say some of the strangest things at the oddest times. All I wanted to know was something about you. And what happens?"

The two of them were affecting each other in a strangely serious, comical, penetrating way. But one thing he did know: they were hitting pay dirt!

They were driving along the beach now, and for the first time he realized how beautiful a night it was. The moon was high and bright. It lighted the breaking waves with flickering outlines of snowy whiteness as they shot up the dark gray sands.

He brought the car to a stop at the side of the road.

"I've always loved the ocean at night," Esther told him. "It has a beauty of something not seen clearly. You don't know exactly what it looks like, but you are sure that it must be beautiful."

They both got out of the car and he walked around the front of it, stepped up next to her and without any thought or plan he reached out and pulled her close.

Their lip met. Silently. Warmly. One explosive, heated embrace. He hadn't planned to kiss her. It was just something that happened—before he even really knew what he was doing. One moment he had been walking toward her. His eyes caught the delicate outline of her profile against the moonlight and then the next moment they were in each other's arms.

Her lips were hot trembling silk, moist and searching. Her tongue nervously reached for him.

The supple and firm and demanding pressure of her body as it crushed against his was fiery-heated lava. It was softness, curving and full. He delighted in the swell of her firm breasts as they pushed on his chest. The pound of her heart. The pressing of her lips and thighs.

The embrace was explosive and electric. He felt every nerve and cell in his body burn hot.

They parted slightly and time froze in vivid series of brilliant flashing colors against the gray of their lives.

He knew at that moment that the woman was going to be more important to him than any other person in the world. Why, he wasn't quite sure. But *somehow* they seemed to know each other as well as two people could know each other.

He had heard of soul mates, yet had never believed in such fantasy ideas until now.

He didn't stop to think. He didn't have to. Lifting her in his arms he carried her out onto the beach, not stopping until they were hidden from the road, near the water's edge. Then, with a gentle ease, he carefully laid her down on the sand.

Their eyes met and their communication was

complete—awareness and need unquestioned. They both wanted the same thing and they were over-whelmed with desperate desire building out of the same mutually shared flaming, violent pressure.

This wasn't just a natural moment of desire. This wasn't seduction. This wasn't anything but pure reality. As simple as breathing. It was one of those moments two people could share without doubting the perfection of it—which two people knew instinctively that they had been created to ex-perience. It was a vital part of their living existence. This moment—the first intimate sharing; this life-long truth each had been awaiting from the moment of birth. This was both the ending of something and the beginning of living.

He moved down to her and the mountain erupted into being. It was a mountain that contained the elements of passion, lust, sexual desire, animal need and something else that could not be so easily fathomed. But just as strongly bound to the other's emotions and passions, as their bodies were finally united in the searing heat of their frantically excited lovemaking.

They blended together, rhythmically, heatedly and physically until the burn and the ache and the overwhelming emotions finally subsided and like an ocean wave, returned to their native home.

For him it was a coming to the point in his life that gave it full meaning. They seemed joined in some soul-like fashion that made their movements, the actions of their bodies, almost meaningless. They were puppets yanked by invisible strings linked to something far deeper within both of them. Everything was on a feeling level so deeply penetrating into his very inner being that he knew this was why he had been given life in the first place.

It was like surfing on nothing but emotion and their physical beings just blended, flowed together into one unified reality. Together like this they became one total creature. It was like two halves becoming one. Now they were whole.

☿ NINE ☿

For Esther, the drive home seemed like a fantastic dream—a fantasy. How could it be real? The whole evening after Norton "rescued" her from the brutal impact of Ken's fist. It was magic.

She had waited in numbed terror, expecting to feel the impact of that fist and then things seemed to happen in a series of speedy events. The walk. The conversation. The drive. All had blended into one. All seemed to be just part of a whole—a small part. The important things happened the moment she stepped out of the car and walked around in front of it right into Norton's impulsive kiss.

From the way it took place, and the wildly unexpected results, it told her a lot about Norton and herself.

The build-up had been, for her, at least, the drive to the beach. The conversation and the laughter. But most of all her sidelong glances in his direction. The excited thrill which had slowly built in herself. Part of her reaction was simply that this was Jamie Norton. That was her first reaction. It was actually the least important. What moved her most was the fact that there seemed to be some kind of mental similarity between them. They both were able to react to the same words, thoughts and ideas.

They both seemed to be aware of this inner communication which said so much and told so much. Then there was the more basic animal attraction.

And there was, in the car, that determination which she had already made up her mind about. Jamie Norton would be the first man she would consciously seduce for the sole purpose of getting her first break.

But that first kiss destroyed that illusion completely. She knew, from that moment on, that she would give in to him for one reason only. She wanted to. Regardless and for no personal gain, except the physical need to be made love to by the most important man in the world.

She liked that. She liked the idea that he knew when to move, when to take the opportunity offered him! Then he moved with a swift determination, without any thought that she wouldn't be willing. So sure of himself. So sure of the two of them. So sure of her need, wanting, her own desperate hunger.

He placed her on the sand and then slid down beside her. The next kiss was the real first one. It was the first of many that built up the physical passion and desire in her to an overwhelming need which possessed her every nerve, muscle and cell. She felt the tender and then furious caressing of his hands as they searched over her body, pulling aside her clothes piece by piece until she was naked to his touches and kisses. And caresses. Oh, his lovely, soft, velvet touches. His lovely moist kisses that flowed over her again and again, continually urging her very soul upwards into a surging peak of desire.

Then he moved against her with a rhythmic drive and motion. It was musical. It was like a concert directed by a godlike conductor. It was as if he could reach into her very inner core and fire it to such red-hot fury that nothing else counted, existed. Nothing was left but the sensations they were both sharing. The heated action of his body against hers was a burning agony that whipped her mind in a tortured painful passion. She heard her voice cry out in the night, moaning for the final union that would make them one. Her whole body ached with the heated need, she felt tremors and the nervous burns run through her like rippling waves of agony.

Desperately she pressed up tighter to him, crying in a low moaning whimper to be taken, to be kissed. Her breasts were fiery with need. Then she felt him lower slowly, as in a never-ending heavenly penetration into her very soul. She felt the fullness of him being enveloped within her, and every nerve fired to literally swallow him whole, everything that was Jamie Norton, the man, the total being of him, the very elements of his soul. She wanted all of him within her. She wanted to literally surround his total being. And never let him escape. She wanted him forever captured within her very being.

Afterwards they lay silently for a long time, half holding the other in their arms. Their breathing slowly became normal; their passion-charred minds cooled; the animal-lusts subsided.

"This is not what I'd really planned," she heard him say in a low, still, husky voice.

"I know."

"No. Not really." He moved away from her and sat up, looking down into her eyes. "I really didn't have any plans of any kind."

"It wouldn't have mattered." She wanted to tell

him that she had been going to let him have her anyway. But the words wouldn't come out, even though she knew that he might understand their meaning. A girl couldn't admit to any man that she was just like him; that her needs were just as strong; and that her desires just as overwhelming. She had to play some kind of silly social game of get me if you can! But she had wanted him. Deep down in the very raw center of her very soul. And wanted him on a raw, nakedly lustful way—animal passion. You couldn't tell a man that, because he liked to believe that it was his male "self" that was doing the seducing in such an overwhelming matter that a woman who should say "no, no!" would, instead, scream "yes." It was the foolish rule of the mating game and there just wasn't any escaping it. Say 'no' when you mean 'yes'.

Oh, god he had been wonderful!

She wanted to scream to him: I want more, again and again, never stop loving me like that—take me any time you want...I'm there for you, for your touches, for your kisses, for your body. For your very soul. Oh, God I'll do anything for you. I'll worship the very ground you walk on. Oh, God, you were so wonderful. I just love you! Love you so much.

That was something a woman never dared say to a man. Not even to herself. Especially one she had only known for a few hours. One who had taken her to the beach and literally banged the hell out of her body. She was a quick pickup in his eyes. A fast chick on the make. A cheap little starlet trying to play the casting couch game. She must be in his eyes nothing more than a slut, tramp, vamp, whore, easy lay.

And she didn't give a bloody damn!

And she knew, somehow, instinctively, that Jamie Norton just couldn't think of her in that way. That part of her wanted to believe this might be so. But how could he feel like she did?

The union of their bodies had almost been soul mating. They had become one in more than a sexual union of bodies.

But, perhaps, this was all illusion—wishful thinking, dreaming on her part. He was a celeb, famous person, and she was nothing but a beautiful body. He'd known many beautiful women just like her. He could hardly consider her different, meaningful, important. Just another easy make.

And there were women like Lilly, who stood on the same level as Jamie Norton. Why would he think of taking an unknown seriously?

It was fantasyland for her. But what a beautiful one.

They had talked a lot after that. About herself and about him. She had told about her own struggles to break into show-business; and about her inner desire to express herself creatively. Her years as a vocal student. Her dramatic lessons. She had touched upon everything that dealt with the matter of Hollywood, acting and singing and getting into a tough racket. The getting nowhere fast.

He had told her about his trouble with his agent

"When I walked out old Manny..."

"Manny?" She felt a sharp dig grind through her at the name. "Manny Anson?"

"You know him?" he asked, surprise showing on his face.

"A bit. He hit on me last night. He tried to get me to go up to his room. Laid it right on the line. Come up and we'll talk about it tomorrow." She laughed then -because of all that had taken place since the evening before. "I told him to go to hell!"

"You're kidding?" The sound of his voice had the edge of disbelief to it. Admiration. "Not to Manny?"

"Why not? It was early. He said that he had some business matters to take care of later on. He was quite blunt about it!"

"Guess he was."

"As it turns out, if I hadn't walked out on him, I'd never come to the party tonight. And then not met you."

That thought left them silent for a long time.

"I'll see you tomorrow?" he asked, after a long time, breaking the quiet.

She nodded. She would see him tomorrow, and the next day, and the next after that. If it was up to her. Not because he was Jamie Norton, big-time star, but because he was a man she liked a lot. Liked more than she could have ever imagined.

Anyway, from what he told her about himself, he wasn't the big-time star he had appeared at first. He thought of himself as a washed-up has-been, who was just getting a chance to pull himself out of the mire of his own making.

When he had come to that part of the story he had paused. "Maybe not my own making—"

The words were more spoken to himself than to her, and she had the definite idea that he wasn't even aware that he had said them out loud. After a moment he shook his head and then stood. "About

98

time you got home."

It was an abrupt cut of mood. As if somehow he had to get rid of her for the time being—anyway. She responded, because she realized that whatever his reasons, they had to be good and valid ones.

"I don't know about tomorrow for sure," he had told her as they drove back toward the Delcado estate. "There are a couple of things I have to take care of."

She had let the matter lie where he dropped it.

Something utterly fantastic had happened on the beach. For her it was the beginning of a totally knew world, new experience. She had no idea what would follow, but only knew she was helpless to do anything less than scramble after this wonderful man. Silly, foolish as it might seem, she was desperately taken by him. It was more than sex. It was more than fame. It was more than anything she had ever known in the past. It was selfless on her part. She just wanted to be a part of his life for as much as it was possible to have him. No matter how small. If this was all there was, that would be enough. If it could last longer, even a lifetime, it would never be long enough to satisfy her now limitless cravings for what they had just shared.

That was an experience no other man would ever be able to give her.

She was convinced of that. Well, at least a large part of her embraced that fantasy. The harder part attempted to distance herself from that and seek a more realistic reality.

And what was left was a frantic, wild, heady, drunken confusion.

The soundly practical side of her said to just ride

with the punches and don't make a life and death thing out of it. She'd just been with a fantastic lover, and that should, really, be the beginning and end of it all.

Sure. Of course.

But she had to be realistic.

* * * * * * *

After he left Esther Vivian, Norton walked into the huge house. The party noise was as loud as it had been earlier when he had left. Noisier—if that was possible.

Things would be swinging until some time in the morning, after the sun had started up across the sky. That was the way all these parties ended. A lot of drunks and hangers-on still boozing it up. Most of the bedrooms filled with men and women; some of them filled with couples who had had their fun; and might still be having it.

He was glad he had taken the care to lock his room up. He didn't feel like walking in and finding a bunch of naked and half-naked sex-hungry drunks stretching out on his bed and couches and on the floor.

Not that he planned on using his room for a while yet. First he wanted to see Lilly, if that was possible. If not her, then Williams or Delcado.

He had waste enough time already.

That thought froze. Bad conclusion. The time spend with Esther had been the most important hours in his life. But that was a totally different issue.

That was special. More than sexual passion. It

had reached into something totally different within his being which simply left him somewhat dazed. But it was more like fantasy.

This was reality. Hard, harsh reality had to be dealt with in a realistic way.

The events of the last couple of days were stunning.

And the last hours, even without the confusion of Esther, were overwhelming.

Now he had to deal with real life, as it really was, as it soon would be.

Meeting George Kayne, along with the drinks, had left him with an unsure feeling concerning all of this suddenly bright deal with Delcado. The club would help Kayne. Managing the two clubs would give him a chance to help a lot of friends and struggling young people to get ahead. Sure. That was all true.

But now his brain was washed clean of all the numbing effects of liquor by the explosive desire and passion and physical excitement of Esther's body. That had helped him to slowly pull out of the drunken haze and return to the center of his problems.

One thing he could say about Esther, she knew how to use her body. Her lips. Silky and moist. The darting nervousness of her tongue as it eagerly met his. The easy response of her every muscle as it excitedly moved to his touch. The soft swell of her delicate but full breasts as his hands had glided over them. Firm and supple. Her flat stomach and smooth rounded thighs and legs. His fingers had explored every hollow and curve and delightedly arranged inch of her thrashing and squirming body. She was

101

one hell of a bundle of lunging action than never stopped moaning with pleasure. So responsive to his touch. So lovely. So much more than he could have ever imagined possible.

She had overwhelmed him in such a way that he simply couldn't fully understand his reaction. That was somewhat unnerving and frightening. Yet so wonderful!

All that had helped to boil away the fuzz of too much liquor. The remaining heady feeling had faded slowly into nothingness, leaving only the conscious awareness that he had a million questions needing solid answers.

He was anxious to get on with his investigation, of why, what and who was responsible for his having been chosen by Delcado to front for a "nice little racket."

Something smelled about it. Terribly. Until he had his solutions—he would continue to feel uneasy about the whole deal.

He had to find out. Lilly might know. If she didn't, then maybe Williams. But first, it had to be Lilly. From there he would know where to go and how to handle matters. He had to find somebody who might know where Lilly might be found. George Kayne was a first stop for that.

He walked through the crowd, which seemed now twice as thick as it had been when he had walked out with Esther.

Finally he made it to the area where the combo had been playing.

"What's new?" Kayne asked.

"Seen Lilly?" He tried to make it sound casual.

"Sure. Sure thing. She was around about twenty

minutes ago. Looking for you."

"Where'd she go?"

"Said something about running up to your room."

Christ, he thought, after the way he'd walked out on her, brutally, almost savagely, turned her down flat, it would seem as if she'd be in a killing mood, rather than a loving one.

Lilly must have wanted to see him for some good purpose. But what?

She wasn't one to waste her time for no reason.

He only hoped that it wasn't just another try at seduction. If he hadn't been interested before making love to Esther, he'd never be interested now, after what had just taken place.

"Thanks," he mumbled over his shoulder, moving off across the room. Finally he found a man in a uniform who was part of the household help.

"You know what room Miss Lilly Benton has?"

"She was looking for you, Mr. Norton," the man said.

"Well, where is she, then?"

"In your room. I let her in. She said she would wait there for you." There was a strange glint in the man eyes. It was the kind of look a person would expect a servant to give when he thinks a lady is waiting in the master's chambers.

Which was completely ridiculous in the case Lilly. It had to be after the brush off he'd given her earlier. Women like her had been known to commit murder for fewer reasons!

Only with Lilly, though, there was a very good chance that things were quite different. They'd been friends for a very long time; been through a lot together. Maybe that made the difference.

He walked up the stairs to the second floor, down the hall toward his bedroom, reached for the knob, found it locked, and then unlocked it with his key. He opened the door. "Lilly, you there?"

He didn't have to hear her answer. She was there all right. Lying on his bed, stark naked.

Christ! He thought. That's all he needed. Lilly on the make! Again. The woman could be one hell of a pain! One hell of a seductive package that half the men in America and the world would give their left nut to possess. And there she was, in the wholly stark!

ᵧ TEN ᵧ

Lilly still had the most beautifully voluptuous body he had ever known. Norton just stood there looking at her for a long time, taking in the sensually bulging shape of her breasts, which were large and beautiful, larger than they ever looked when hidden by a dress. She had the fullest breasts he had ever seen on a woman, the large, rigid pink nipples seemed to be eagerly waiting for a man's caresses and kisses and lips.

He watched fascinated as her hand slipped down a long her legs, caressing and nervously pressing. Even though his own passionate energy was completely drained by the session with Esther he couldn't help responding to the raw, suggestive quality of Lilly's actions and the convulsive ripple of excitement that moved through her body.

One look at her half closed eyes and he could see the glassy sheen of alcoholic haze. Lilly was nothing but the wonderful little hottie he had first known years before. The woman who had become a big star by sleeping her way up to fame. Actually, as they had laughed about it: up in flame! Raging hot, passionate flame. In bed she was a deliciously wild whore. And that he had liked about her. A woman should be a "whore" in bed. It was because of her

raw and savage passions that he had originally become so interested in her. That was early on. They
were making a love scene for one of his movies.
Usually when two professionals kissed on the set
they only touched lips. This embrace was open-
mouthed and tongues searching as all hell. She just
parted her lips and her tongue surged eagerly into
his. It was enough to get him interested in conclud-
ing matters later in the privacy of his own apartment. And there she'd pressed his lips into her fantastic breasts, moving him from nipple to nipple in
greedy, surging hunger, as if not getting enough of
such frantic stimulation. Her hips had rammed up
against his, her thighs parted and captured the hurting hard she had so instantly inspired. She acted as
if it wasn't possible to get enough. Her hips just
lifted up and enveloped him totally. She almost savagely "raped" his body that first time. Later they'd
taken it very slowly, devouring one another, savor-
ing every moment with greedy hunger.

"Baby, love man!" she cooed, "Come to
mother!" Her arms reached out toward him.

Even in such a drunken condition Lilly was an
attractive woman. Narrowly pinched waist; large
curvaceous hips; rounded, heavy, but beautifully
shaped legs. Men found a very desirable woman.

But he didn't want her this way. In fact, he
didn't want to cheapen the experience he'd just
shared with Esther so short a time ago on the beach.

She squirmed in anxious anticipation as he
moved toward the bed. Her lips parted and her
tongue moistened their surface. One of her hands
ran along hip and thigh, the fingers digging violently into the flesh. It was an action learned under

106

both real film direction and then later used in private to seduce a man. She was a very skilled seductress.

"Oh, Jamie, come and give me…give it to me. I want to…have you in me. I need it," she moaned in a very convincing voice. "I want my hot hard lover."

She had used that kind of come-on so many times in the past. It was quite an act, quite erotic, even though he experienced the show so many times in the past in its many variables. She could be deliciously vulgar.

Strangely enough her words didn't slur; they were well formed, controlled. "I want to feel you deep inside me, Jamie. Like before…like we've always been."

She squirmed, parted her thighs wide, in blatant invitation. "Right here, honey! Right there!" she moaned in open desire, eyes half closed. "Right down here."

Her fingers ran between her legs, then upwards, deeply caressing herself. "Right in here, just like you love me to squeeze all around you when you're inside me. Oh…Jamie, remember how good it is? I can get so tight around you. Remember?"

He stood there, feeling mixed emotions, but not the raw, naked desire she wanted to inspire. She had such a fantastic body and was so passionate in her love-making. But that was all a part of the past for him. He really didn't want to play that game any more. Not will her.

She frowned, froze, suddenly aware of his lack of response. "Damn it, can't you service an old lover? I need it, really."

He didn't moved, just continued to stare at her.

He simply didn't know what to do or say. Anything he would say would be more damaging, hurtful. And he didn't want to hurt Lilly. Never that.

"It's her, isn't it?" she snapped, furious. "That little slut!"

"Cut it out, Lil. You have no right!" he retorted more angrily they he'd meant to sound. "Knock it off!"

"Oh, Christ!" she blurted, furious. "I can't believe it!"

"Please, Lil. We've been friends too long."

"A friend would screw me to orgasm right now! Not do me like this! Damn you!"

"Lil. Please, try to understand."

She considered him for a moment, then said: "You fucked her, didn't you?"

He shrugged, helplessly. What could he say?

"Why do you want that blonde little bitch when you can have little old sexy Lilly!" she blurted out in a nasty, throaty voice. "Tell me that!"

Then she paused, softened a little, said: "Come on, love, give me a bit of you…I really do need it. I hurt down here…I want you filling me."

Only Lilly could beg like that and only with him. Strangely their friendship had shattered far beyond ego a long time ago. She wasn't hurt so much as frustrated. Being turned down by him was not an ego thing. She really did have an overpowering sexual drive.

"No dice!" He stood at the edge of the bed, looking down. Lilly was beautiful enough, but nothing like Esther. "Really, Lil. Let it cool."

She ignored the meaning behind his words. "Come down to baby! Baby wants a man! Baby needs a man right down here, deep inside, just screwing her like crazy. You can't have forgotten how good I am!"

Lilly had been a real good partner; the affair had been a passionately high point in his life. What attraction she had once had was gone now. She was a beautiful body that a man might service, but that was all.

Yet, this was the first time he realized the truth about their split up as lovers. It hadn't been Lilly but rather something in him. He should have realized the truth earlier.

How long she had been waiting for him, wanting and desiring, he had no way of knowing. The earlier turn-down hadn't meant a thing to her. And that, really, wasn't too much of a surprise. She had no ego with him. But for a moment he couldn't help feeling a deep pain at the knowledge that he might hurt her. That was one thing he never would really want to do.

"I'm sorry. Lilly."

It didn't sink in.

Lilly just smiled, and came at him like a soft, lovely demon from the very pits of fiery hell.

He just stood there, unmoving, not resisting, helpless to step away.

She raised up to him, her arms sliding around his neck and her lips savagely bruising his, open and moist. He felt the violent rough dampness of her tongue attempting to move forcefully past his teeth. He couldn't control the animal reaction that caused his own lips to part and give open freedom for her to probe the darting action of her kiss into his in mouth.

Like a puppet she was mastering him, pulling all the right strings.

Her full eager breasts pressed hard against his chest, squirming and rhythmically matching the upward surge and churning of her hips.

"Come on, lover man!" she challenged. "Bet you can get hot fast!"

She grabbed at his groin, expertly finding the triggers she had memorized so long before. She knew just where to fire him beyond control.

"That's it baby," she moan in pleasure. "Hard as a rock, you is! Love my baby so hard like that."

He couldn't stop now, even if he wanted to. Lilly knew exactly how to excite his more basic drives and desires. He was like a sexual instrument that she had mastered. He simply didn't, couldn't, care any longer about her feelings, about anything. She had him totally helpless. All he could think of was floating on the sensations that her passion hungry body could inspire.

There wasn't any waiting. It was the brutal and direct action that she demanded, and he didn't have the will to stop or resist. He'd tried to check his action only for a second.

"I don't want...want this!" he breathed heavily in her ear.

"Yes you do, honey. What's in my hands, that's wanting all of me around you. So...big and hard."

"Lil...please." He wanted to stop—yet her fingers kept instantly holding him.

He kept telling himself to walk away, step back, to stop her, but his body just didn't listen.

Her face pulled back an inch and she looked seductively into his eyes.

110

"You are so good to have…like this!" she almost sobbed, digging her fingers into his back. "So…good!"

That was it. He couldn't stop. He didn't want to any more.

She literally dragged him down on the bed, between her legs, fingers directing, shifting and then releasing him as she lifted up so her body could envelop all that she had been holding. Now he was wrapped in a fiery vice that would not let him go. Her legs held him firmly in place as they began the savage dance of passion. She literally clawed at his whole body with her whole body. It was savage, two beasts grinding at one another until nothing moved in their final moments of ecstatic pleasure.

Then afterwards they lay next to each other exhausted. Then once they had rested she turned and pulled him nearer to her.

Her lips smiled. Her eyes sparkled and her mouth opened as her tongue darted outwards.

"I just knew you wanted me. I knew we'd be like this. All night…we can be like this all night!" She reached for his hands and placed, the on her breast. "Oh, God, Jamie, you feel good holding them like that."

But it did nothing to him this time. It was just completely finished.

"Stop it, Lilly!" he, demanded, pulling his hands away from her body and standing up. "Cut, it! Get dressed."

"Your turn homo?" she laughed, "or did I drain you out!" in a high pitched voice. Then she saw the drained, harsh reality in his eyes. He was serious. And she saw that.

"Screw you!"

She stood and walked across the room. With each step her hips jerked angrily and sensually. Then she picked up her clothing, which was lying on a chair.

She was just raw sex. Sex was sex. She's just proven how easily she could seduce him. All a woman had to do was shove her body at a man in the right way and his groin would groan with hot desire. And Lilly was one of those women who knew all the tricks. And she had just proven it.

It was funny how many things he was seeing clearly for the first time. Maybe it was because he was looking for the first time.

Show business had its good sides to it; he had seen some of them only through the foggy haze that had blinded him to its defects. And there were plenty of defects. It seemed like he had hit most of them.

Overdrinking, living it up. Too much success too quickly. Behind the scenes money pay-offs so that he would get the key spots. Manny Anson had been good at getting good deals for him because he *bought* them. The people with talent didn't get much of a chance when some guy could pull strings and pay off big shots for his own people. But that was the name of the game. Who you know; who could yank chains; who opened doors.

Lilly was almost dressed by then. It was taking her a lot longer than normal because of two basic facts: she was slightly gassed and shaking mad! Or so it seemed.

But he realized, suddenly, that it was all part of a game she wanted to playact out. Drama for dramatics. Nothing more.

"Cut the playacting, Lilly!" he ordered, stepping over to where she was standing and arranging her dress over the full swell of her breasts.

"No man ever turned me down before!" Raw fury was showing in her eyes. "Twice in one night!"

"That's not true. You balled me wild. Anyway, that's not what's bothering you. And you know it!"

"Know...*what*?"

"It's been through with us for a long time. So stop acting like you're hurt. You won your point. I got sucked in. But...stop the game playing. You were just trying to prove something to yourself that didn't need proving."

"That little blonde bitch!" she spat out, angrily. But there was an edge of amusement to her words. Was she laughing at him? Or just covering up some inner fury?

"Knock it, Lilly!" He stepped closer to her, taking told of her shoulders. His hands squeezed, lightly on them. "We're beyond jealous crap. You should be happy for me."

"Don't touch me!"

"Cut it!"

"Don't you dare!" She glared at him very dramatically. "Let go of me, you brute!"

That as right out of a script.

When he didn't release her, she struggled to be free of him. Her body squirmed violently, her face twisting with every action. He didn't let go.

"Oh, you delicious beast! How thrilling. Are you going to ravish me, now? Oh, yes. Please do."

"Slow it down!" He realized that Lilly was having more fun than she ever would have had in bed;

and she was making the most of it. Some people were like that; they liked scenes so much that they would go out of their way to create them, just for the fun of it. That was Lil.

One slap was all that was needed. He swung.

She gave out a yell of shock. Her face turned from red to white. A startled whimper pushed out from narrowed lips,

"You're serious!" she sighed in a low, rasping voice.

Her eyes frowned and she stepped back a couple of inches.

That was show business.

A bunch of overgrown kids. Play acting.

A bunch of stupid, selfish, children playing in an adult's sandbox which contained deadly traps under the surface.

And they had both fallen right into those lovely, seductive, claw-like traps!

114

ELEVEN

Some people didn't mature emotionally until it was too late. Lilly was one. She lived in a world of false glamour and famed glitter and lies; and she had made the fatal mistake of believing them. He had done this same thing and only today was he slowly beginning to claw his way out of that false fantasy.

Lilly's expression had changed once more. It was serious. And for the first time since he had known her, it was slightly honest looking-almost childlike. It had a real appeal to it.

"Lil, I'm sorry."

"Forget it!" she stated, evenly. "I deserved it. You're right, we've been friends for too long. Screw ego. There are a lot of men I can get…and it was a dirty trick coming on to you like that. I knew just where to fire you up…"

"Yes. You sure did!" he confessed in a warm, tender voice.

She laughed. "You sure looked surprised when I got you all hot and bothered there!"

"I didn't think I had it in me any more. I mean…tonight."

"Don't rub it in, Honey! A girl has just so much…well, what ever it is that runs our egos."

"Funny how things happen…a lot of things have happened today that'll get me thinking, Lil. Maybe you can give me some answers to a few questions."

"Anything, Jamie." Her eyes looked down at her hands. "I'm sorry. I must have looked and acted like a real bitch."

"I guess we all acted that way. Or most of us. Maybe that's why we get into this racket. Make-believe. The world of fantasy. Nobody grows up, but instead they live in a world that never really exists except in the vision of their imaginations and the imagination of the press agents. The silver screen shadows which never really live."

"It's funny, that slap you gave me…suddenly I saw you were so deadly serious…and if you were serious, then as a real friend, well, then, maybe I should…back off… try to help. Does that make sense?"

"I don't know quite where to begin." He shrugged. Then started shooting blindly, "How come Delcado picked on me?"

She looked up into his eyes. The expression on her face was closer to a frown of concern than anything.

"What's it to you, Jamie?" Each word held the sound of terror and dread.

"I want out!"

She took in a deep breath of shock. "No! Don't! You can't walk out on Delcado."

"Why not?"

"We can't escape. Me or you!" she told him. "This isn't a game, Jamie. And they have us, lock stock and body. Sold and paid for. There simply isn't any way out!"

116

Her reaction was fitting in perfectly with what he was sure must be the hard facts.

"I was set up for this deal. Wasn't I?"

Her face silently said yes.

"A long time ago. When Manny forced me to walk out on him! Right?"

Her silence confirmed his statement.

The more he talked the madder he was feeling inside. The tight, agonizing fury he'd held back for so many months was finally starting to ebb out.

"I've been thinking all day. Certain things have become apparent that I never had seen before. Guess because I never looked closely at them before to-day." He started walking the length of the room. "I just reacted, running from bottle to bottle, fancy broad to cheap slut."

He was vaguely aware that a lighted cigarette was in his hands, but he didn't remember having taken it out and lighting it. "Delcado was behind Manny, wasn't he?"

She nodded. Her eyes were looking down at the floor.

"Delcado has been behind me all along. I see that now. It all fits so nicely—"

"It's to late to do anything about it now"

He turned towards her. "Why?"

She looked at him. Her eyes didn't move from his. Her face was white and tense looking. Her lips moved as if she had no control over what they said- as if they spoke against her will. "You don't know these people like I do. They're big. Too big for just one man or even a group of men to fight. You can't beat them; you can't walk out on them. If you think what happened after you walked out on Manny was

117

a show of their strength and power, you have another think coming. They don't care about people.
We're just pawns to play around with. They look
around, see who is there, and then they play them.
And actors are, well, cheap whores. We'll all sell
our soul for a chance at fame. Well, the ones these
monsters own. You think the casting couch is a dirty
mattress to be fucked on? Well, that's nothing com-
pared to what these people do. They play for keeps.
And they play for fun. But it is all a deadly game to
them. And our lives mean nothing. If we play along,
they continue to reward us monkeys on the string. If
we screw around with the rules, they just cut the
strings and let you fall into the gutter or graveyard.
And they don't even notice! They wouldn't stop
short of killing you or anybody who stood in their
way. Delcado didn't get all this for being a nice little boy. He'd just as soon kill you as swat a fly; and
it would take less effort."

She stopped finally, for breath.

"They set this up a long time ago," she continued after a moment. "They wanted to open a club
with a big name, fronting for it. There was little
chance of getting anybody unless they were set up
for the deal. From the way Delcado looked at it, a
big name star didn't need the money, and a small-
timer wouldn't be big enough to do him any good.
You were ideal. A drinking fool with a short fuse
who was playing at the game, on the edge—and not
very stable. They figured you'd be easy to dump for
a while, then pick you up when you're desperate
and hungry. Even then, that wasn't the only thing.
Delcado is slightly wildly, insanely, a mad-hatter
psychotic! The idea of making and breaking men

118

and women is his big charge and thrill. A thrill a minute, too. He's so bloody evil." She spat that last out with total contempt. "You don't know what evil is until you meet up with a power-pig like him. You can't imagine what he can do to a woman."

"Take it easy, Lil."

"No…you don't know…. Take Mable…you know her, don't you?"

She paused, and after he nodded, went on: "Well I heard about her little escapade with you this afternoon. You're just lucky that you didn't do any-thing with her…. You wouldn't recognize what she looks like now. I came on her by accident…" Her voice choked violently and her eyes moistened. "I wouldn't want to live if I were her."

She shook herself and then said: "But that's some-thing else. The thing is Delcado liked the idea of taking a big star and ruining him. Power in the palm of his fat hand. It was all a part of a wonderful power game to him. He could sit back and watch, like some bloody producer creating a film—but this was real life with real people and real hopes and real dreams and real fucking hell! He simply creamed you like a piece of bread. He smeared you and dumped you. And then waited out a time-period while you simply sank deeper and deeper. He watched the money dwindle and the price drop for the whores and booze you could afford. He waited for the right time to pick you up out of the dirt as he calls it. Yes. And he laughed heartily at you and about you. And that hurt me, too. He's so evil you can't imagine."

"Blackballed," he cursed inwardly, feeling sick. But suddenly that word had little meaning against

119

what she was telling him.

"That's about it, Jamie. He buys and sells bodies. That's all he really likes to do. You're a body. Nothing more. A non-person. I'm a body. And he owns both of us. To the hilt. What real power he has is really only over people like us. They are afraid of him and rightfully terrified. He wanted a big time star. A name they could use. They wanted a person who might, under the right conditions, go along with them. You were a perfect choice. So they picked you. You looked like a stooge for that part and they were right. Drinking too much was the sign of weakness that hung you. You had a good temper, and most of all—which you didn't know—you were already on your way down the ladder."

That one came as a blow below the belt. But some-how it didn't hurt as much as he might have thought. Maybe that was because it simply didn't matter anymore. Fame wasn't the most important thing. He was already used to the truth that he was "out," so the blow was softened by that fact.

"If there had ever been a perfect fall guy, you were it. So, Manny got orders to push you. It was easy. You push easy. Then the carpet was pulled out from under you." She was silent for a long moment. "I didn't know it at the time. It was later; several months after we returned to the States and were finished with each other."

Her voice faded out then.

"The cold-blooded little damn bastards!" He was more than just sick or mad. The temper and heated fury were controlled. Just the sickness gnawing at his insides was something that he could not stop. "What right do they have using people like

120

pawns on a chess board? Bodies for sale—that's the game they play...who wants a new body for sale?"

"They'll kill you if you try to walk out on them!"

"Oh, to hell with that!"

"They'd kill me if they found out I told you this!" She stood and walked over to him. "So you see why you can't walk out now?"

He just felt cold inside. He didn't know what he wanted to do. He hadn't realized how it really was. He'd guessed some of the truth. But he had never guessed that one human being could be so cold-blooded about controlling others.

For no good reason but the fact that Delcado liked to play games with people's lives, they were in an ugly trap. "I don't know what I'm going to do, Lilly."

A sigh breathed out from her lips; it had started from her chest—a sigh that held fear and terror and hopelessness.

"What would happen if we went to the police. Couldn't they do anything?"

She just looked blankly at him.

"Isn't there anything that can be done? People don't have the right to...control others like this...own our souls!"

"They take the right. Weak bastards like us give them the right. They can sell and buy people like us by the dozens, without even having to look for them. Just snap their fingers. They have the right, because they can kill you if you try to take it away from them. They'll kill and get away with it, believe me!"

"But..."

121

"But they already have!"

He looked at her for a long time after that. For the first time he saw lines of living fear as if she had lived for a long time with a heavy burden on her shoulders. As if she really hadn't been the gay fantasy-filled screen sweetheart. He realized then, that she had never really been the immature person that she appeared.

How could she be? Not with such facts hanging over her very life.

"So darling," she smiled, patting him on the cheek. "You won't do anything about it?"

He didn't really know. There didn't seem to be anything a person could do. But there had to be! He didn't want to stay in that shadow land....

He wanted out! And now! But how?

How?

People like this were dangerous. What if they got a politician in their clutches like this? What kind of monsters ruled Washington D.C.? Were men like Delcado there, pulling invisible strings at the White House, controlling the leaders of the land? Certainly show business was small potatoes next to the political game. The power brokers were everywhere. Some were caring, powerful people who wanted to do nothing but help mankind. But there were the Delcados who feasted on owning people. Just for the pleasure of owning them.

Suddenly he realized that he was very much alone.

Lilly was gone.

Thoughtfully, he moved over to the bar. Poured himself a drink, downed it in one gulp and poured another.

He had to decide what to do. Should he take the path of easy money? Or take the chance of being killed? And getting a lot of other innocent and not so innocent people knocked around.

And maybe killed, too.

That's what he had to make up his mind about— and it wasn't going to be easy. No matter which way he moved it was a deathtrap.

BODIES 4 SALE, BY CHARLES NUETZEL

℣ TWELVE ℣

Norton started drinking one shot of whiskey after another. He didn't think about what he was doing. Instead, he was thinking about what he was going to be doing. What he knew he had to do, regardless of what it cost.

He couldn't let Delcado ruin his life for good. If he didn't find some way out of this deal, then it could become fatal.

Law was law. It was one thing to be a wise guy and make a quick buck by outsmarting some other person. But it should be done legally. Business was business. But it was another thing when you went beyond the law to make money. And now he realized he didn't want anything to do with this deal.

He had to be careful, though. One mistake could be the end of his life and maybe a couple of friends might get hurt in the meantime.

That was what really got him more than anything else did—Delcado, a man who thought he could run people around, just for his own pleasure and fun. Personal gain. Mental kicks. The damn little bastard!

The glass that had been in his hand suddenly flung through the air smashing against the wall. There was a popping sound as it shattered into a crumbled mass of broken glass and dripping liquid that made a jagged pattern of moisture on the wall and floor.

That's what he needed. Something to ease over the mental confusion and resistance to—to what?

It was one thing to think about doing something—and quite another to be doing it. If he blew his top, tried to walk out on this deal, chances were that he'd find himself dead, or pretty near it.

That damn little bastard!

He took another strong swallow. The liquor flowed down his throat, hitting his stomach and quickly ebbing its effect up through his nervous system and into his head.

Buzz, buzz. Bastard Delcado!

The world was spinning in a series of shapeless phantoms. Shadows full of half reality and half thoughts. It was a world of mind-twirling emotions conjuring up pictures of a gigantic Delcado reaching down for him, the fingers wrapping tightly around his body and after lifting upward toward the sky, the man let his hand open and Norton was falling suddenly down towards a staked pit.

The red blur opened up slowly, peeling inwards and then rapidly fading away The world of reality was surrounding him on every turn.

At first he didn't know where he was. Then he recognized things. Somehow he'd walked out of his room, down a flight of steps, and was now standing in the large hallway that opened into almost every part of the huge mansion. But he was facing the direction of Delcado's private business den.

Why? He didn't know. Vaguely he was aware that his right hand was holding a bottle. He didn't have to look to know what it was—or what it meant. In a blind fury he had walked from his room down the steps and into the hallway, without even knowing what he was doing! Carrying the whiskey bottle all the way.

He saw Williams walking through the hallway, towards the large ballroom where the party was still going fairly strong. Walking over to the man, he called out, "Hey, Williams!"

The swollen prune-man turned.

"What you want?"

The voice held contempt.

Norton held down the impulse to swing the whiskey bottle right at the man's face. Hell, how he already hated the guy's guts!

"Look," he said, in a controlled, even voice. "Where's Delcado?"

"How am I supposed to know?" The man started to move away. Norton reached out for his arm.

Williams turned slowly, his eyes looking at Norton's hand, where it held him.

"Let go!" The words were tight and hard. The eyes squinting and cold. "I said to—let go!"

"Where's Delcado?" Norton didn't budge. His hand stayed exactly where it was, squeezing tighter on the man's arm.

Williams struggled to be free. Then, when he saw it didn't do any good, he looked up at Norton. "I'll tell you, Mister Norton, to let go just one more time."

"Where would I find Delcado?"

For a long time the two of them stood there, staring at each other. Sizing up the opponent. Then Williams' face relaxed a little; but the eyes seemed to squint a bit more. "He might be in his office."

Norton's fingers released the man.

"Your time will come, Mister Bum!" Williams started to take a threatening step forward, then paused. "Your time will come!"

"So, I'm scared to death!"

"Look, I don't like what you done! Just watch your step! I get mine in the end…so shut your mouth!"

"Go to hell!" Norton cursed, turning and walking toward the huge double doors which led to Delcado's private office.

* * * * * * *

George Kayne watched Manny Anson move across the room toward where he was playing a couple of standards with his bass man and drummer. The crowd was already beginning to thin. The time was pretty near three in the morning.

"You might as well break things off now." Manny told him, stepping up to the piano. "Mr. Delcado wants to see you for a moment in his private office. Come with me."

This didn't figure.

"You seen Norton?" Manny asked.

"Yeah. Quite a surprise. I thought he was finished around here, at least!"

"Hell no! He's starting all over again. Gets a real chance to swing things, now. Has a good deal worked up for him. Delcado's two clubs will be fronted by him."

"You kidding?" Kayne exclaimed in surprise. Norton hadn't mentioned anything about them being

Delcado's. "Then—then he's the boss?"

"That's about it, Georgie-boy. The reason why I tried to get you in on the deal—thought the two of you might like working together. Like old-times. Delcado saw something else good about the idea— that's what he wants to talk to you about."

It didn't figure. Why was Manny doing Norton any favors? But this wasn't the time to start demanding answers to any questions. He'd have to ad-lib it!

He finished the number and told the boys to break it up for the night. Then he stood and started to follow his agent across the room.

"What's up, Manny? Give it to me straight!" He couldn't help asking the man as they stepped into a large room lined with floor to ceiling bookcases.

"You'll see."

There were only two people in the room. Manny walked over to the bar centered along one wall. "What a drink?"

"Yeah, could use one. Bourbon."

"Delcado will be around in a moment or so." Manny handed him a drink.

"I've been thinking, Manny."

"Don't. Not right now, kid."

"This   deal.   It   smells   strange.   At least…puzzling."

Manny looked at him for a long time. The stare was icy--surprise. "What you getting at?"

"Well, take Delcado. Why'd he show up last night? He didn't have to. Did he?"

A voice from behind said, "No, I didn't!"

Kayne turned. Delcado was standing there. The man's face was serious. "Look, Mister Piano-man, have a seat!"

The words were a command.

He sat. The chair was stiff and uncomfortable. Delcado settled himself across from Kayne in a large, leather-covered chair. He snapped his fingers.

"A drink, Anson!"

Silence.

If things had smelled rotten before, now they stunk to holly hell.

Manny gave their large host a glass of scotch.

"Okay, piano-man, you want some answers and you're going to get them." The voice was softer now, but Kayne wasn't fooled by this sudden show of friendliness. It was an act which Delcado's narrowed eyes gave away; the eyes remained serious and hard. "You been a friend of Norton's for a long time, haven't you?"

"Sure thing."

"He likes you pretty much, too. That's the reason you're in this thing." Delcado let a silence follow that statement.

"In what?" Kayne asked, feeling a slight coldness creep up his spine.

"Well, you wanted to know why I personally took the time to look you over last night." Delcado sighed deeply as if terribly tired. "Well, it wasn't to hear the keyboard stuff, or your voice. That didn't matter. What I was interested in was sizing you up." He paused and leaned forward. "You look like a smart guy "

Kayne didn't say anything. If he had learned one thing in his life, it was to remain quiet. Listen; say nothing; and just wait. Vamp.

"Well, as you probably now know Norton is set

to front for a couple of night-spots for me. They'll have his name. But what you don't know is that one club will have a gambling casino set-up."

"I don't get it. *Why* are you telling me this?"

"Because that's where you fit in. You're to organize a group for a lounge show. Three or four piece. I don't particularly care what kind show you put on, just as long as it is good."

"Why me?"

"Because of Norton."

"I'm sorry, Mr. Delcado, but I just don't get it."

The big man sighed. "Look, piano-man, I set you up on a deal, and you ask too many questions! What you want? A road map?"

That was just about what he wanted. He didn't like playing guessing games, especially with people like this or with deals like this one. He wanted it in black and white. If it weren't for Jamie being connected, he'd back out right then…

"Look, let's put it this way: You and Norton are good friends. You work well together. He would have hired you the first chance he got. But for the club part. I want you in the casino."

That wasn't the complete answer, he was sure of that. Also he knew that now there was another good reason for his being thrown into the deal.

"What you mean, Mr. Delcado," Kayne pointed out stiffly, "is that if I'm in the casino part Jamie be kept in line can just so much easier. Right? That he might be less inclined to bow out of the whole thing if some of his friends were liable to get hurt. Is that it?"

Delcado laughed.

"Manny, didn't I tell you we have a bright boy,

131

here?" The laughter suddenly stopped as fast as it had begun.

"A real bright boy!"

Delcado looked-directly-into Kayne's eyes, stood and stepped over to him. His right hand tapped on Kayne's chest with every other word. "You get this, Mister Piano-man. And get it good! I want you in because you're going to help keep Jamie in line. He has a temper. You're job is keeping him from backing out! Sell him. Keep it goin' and you keep giggin'—you got me?"

"What if I tell you to go shove it? Like split to hell and back!"

The man's face blanched white. Automatically he stepped back a little. Then he laughed again. This time louder and clearer. "Glad to see you're a great kidder. We need folks like you. A joke a minute. Great on the stage. Great on the keyboard. Just simply wonderful on the mike. Ya got a great voice, sonny boy. We can do some live recordings. Things like that. I heard you love singing the songs. We'll make you a big star. Why not, Manny? Why not?" He didn't wait for an answer. His words had been cold and fast coming. His eyes even colder. "You turn down a deal like that Mister Piano-boy…you do that mister, and you're dead! Not your career, buddy. I'm not talking about no goddamn stupid career. I'm talking about your lousy life. Got me? Dead. In a trench. In a bucket of cement. In like ended—buried alive, bottom of the creek. I don't play games!"

Manny broke in "He means it Georgie. He really means it!" The man's voice had an edge of fear in it.

"Of course he means it!" Jamie Norton's voice

132

shouted from behind them. "He'll kill us all, if we give him the chance. Little Big Man, trying to play God!"

ᵧ THIRTEEN ᵧ

The sound of Norton's words seemed to bounce off the walls, slamming into their ears like a death sentence:

He'll kill us all, if we give him the chance. Little Big Man, trying to play God!

There was a long silence after that, as the other three men slowly turned in Norton's direction,

It was Delcado who spoke first. His voice was silky ice. "What's the trouble, Norton?" The features of his face smiled, but the tight gripping of his hands showed the inner fury.

"Just that you're...."

Manny quickly broke in, his voice high pitched—his eyes wide with terror. "For God's sake, Norton!—Don't! Don't say anything you'll be sorry for..."

"Shut up!" Norton told him, stepping forward. Manny quickly attempted to get between Norton and Delcado. His hands reached an arm's length in front of him, trying to push Norton back.

"Get out of my way, little man!"

Manny shot to one side. It took only one swing of Norton's arm to push the agent out of his way, "Now, Mr. Big Shot, Delcado!" Norton raised the whiskey bottle like a weapon. Some of the liquor still in it dribbled down his arm and onto the floor.

Delcado backed up like a frightened child, "Take it easy, Norton. There's no call to get all worked up...." The man's voice was shaking slightly, his eyes widened. "What's this all about? I'm sure we can work thing's out."

"Shut up! And sit down!"

Manny again: "You don't know what you're doing!"

Norton turned toward the agent. "I told you to shut up!"

Manny froze right where he was.

Delcado was sitting in his large padded chair. "Not there!" Norton cried. He pointed to the rigid one. Delcado didn't move. His face was more relaxed now. The first shocked terror had left. He wasn't afraid anymore. "Now tell me, Jamie..."

"Mr. Norton, to you!"

"Mr. Norton, then." The voice was even and calm. No sign of emotion, either way. Slowly his hands reached into his jacket pocket and pulled out a cigar and lighter. "Now tell me, Mr. Norton. What's the trouble?"

Norton had been breathing rapidly, both from anger and the slight sickening feeling he got when he thought of this greedy little man. Delcado had and wanted the power to control other people's lives!

Norton's emotions suddenly subsided. He was in control. For the moment, at least.

Kayne moved up to him. "Look, Jamie, take it easy."

"You know what kind of a bastard this guy is?" Norton asked.

136

"It's not worth the bother." Kayne's hand reached, for the bottle in Norton's hand. "Give it to me!"

Norton did as he was told.

"What's gotten you all worked up, Mr. Norton?" Delcado asked, lighting the cigar and blowing smoke into the air, "It can't be all that bad."

"Shut up!"

Delcado's eyes squinted, but he remained silent. Norton turned to Kayne. "You know what kind of bastard this guy is?"

"He gave me a pretty good idea." Kayne moved over to the large desk and sat on the edge of it. "But what's your problem?"

Norton needed a drink and he moved over to the bar and mixed one.

"I don't know what I was planning to do," he started to explain to Kayne. "I still don't!"

"Well, "Delcado started to say, "What's the—"

"If you don't mind! Freeze that damned mouth of yours!"

Manny moved, for the first time in minutes. "Norton, please!" You don't know this man like I do."

Delcado's fingers snapped and Manny returned to silence. Cut off like a radio! Norton felt like vomiting.

"I want out, Delcado!"

"What's the problem?"

"You. This whole damned set up. I want out. And as of now!"

Manny moved forward once more. "He won't let you."

Delcado snapped his fingers again. Manny silenced.

"I know about the whole deal. Everything. From beginning to end," Norton announced, holding back his building anger.

"I told you everything." Delcado's voice was smooth, soft, seemingly all innocence.

"I'm afraid you left out a few details." Norton was beginning to feel an angry burn run through him. He turned to his friend, Kayne. "You know what these two slobs did to me?"

Kayne shook his head slowly from side to side. His eyes hadn't once left those of Delcado's.

"They cold-bloodedly sold me out. They planned the whole thing. Just to set up a deal for these two clubs. Just very calmly decided to put an end to my career. And then after almost killing me bringing me back alive in total control of my future. They blackballed me. Sweet little bastards! They make a nice little team don't they?"

"Norton," Manny yelled, "You don't under-stand."

"Oh, be quiet," Delcado snapped, standing up.

"Sit!" Norton ordered.

"I've had just about enough of this. I think that it's about time that *you* sat down. And *right now*!" The big man was moving in his direction.

"You can go to hell!"

"I wouldn't advise doing or saying one more thing!" Williams' voice sounded from the doorway.

All of them turned.

The Delcado trigger-man was standing there, a nasty smile on his face, a small black .38 in his hands. The gun was pointed in Norton's direction. "Do as the man told you. Sit down!"

Norton was aware of two things when Williams entered the room. One: the gun. Two: the man's almost contented anxious grin. As if he were enjoying the fact that he was pointing a deadly gun at Norton.

Then suddenly the whiskey bottle, which Kayne had taken from Norton, flew at Williams. The attack was so unexpected that nobody moved except the gunman. He directed the gun in Kayne's direction and fired.

Then Norton leaped at the furious trigger-man. The bottle struck the guy on the side of the head and it gave Norton a chance to get to him. He let his fists fly.

Everything was like some scene in a movie, only this wasn't planned out for the cameras. This was real life, and the gun didn't have blanks and the men in this room didn't have any moral hang-ups. They would thoughtlessly kill.

But Jamie Norton wasn't without skills of his own. And he lunged with everything in him, every muscle, and nerve, every instant thought. This was play-acting on a real-life scale. And his life depended on a skilled performance. No script. Yet in films, there had been professional lawmen giving direction for fight scenes. And now he drew upon all that.

One ugly blow connected with the man's jaw. Another into the pit of his stomach and a third at the bridge of his nose.

Blood spurted over the broken face. Norton reached for the gun that had fallen on the floor. The man followed his weapon. And Norton kicked him full on the mouth. Redness erupted around the mangled lips as they all but were torn away from the teeth.

Norton stood up, the gun in his hand. "Okay, George, let's get out of here fast!"

Kayne didn't need a second invitation, he moved to Norton's side.

"Hurt bad?" he asked the musician.

"Nothing, I don't think, anyway."

Delcado raised a hand. "You're dead! Both of you!"

"Go to hell!" Norton told him, moving closer to the door.

"You do that, mister!" Kayne joined in as he followed Norton from the room.

They heard Manny's voice cry over and over again. "He'll kill the both of you, he'll kill the both of you...he'll kill the both of you—"

Norton closed the door and directed Kayne toward the front entrance. "Have a car?"

Kayne directed him while searching for his keys.

When they were in the car driving, Norton turned to Kayne. "Where?"

The other shook his head, painfully. Then his eyes brightened, "Maybe Frankie's. She might help. They would look at my place first thing. They don't...know her..."

It had only taken a short time to get to Frankie's. By then Kayne had weakened quite a bit from the wound in his shoulder. The man had just managed to park the car, then half collapsed over the steering wheel. Norton found it necessary to half carry the smaller man up a flight of stairs to Frankie's apartment.

It had been a few moments before she answered

140

the door and the moment she saw them her mouth went wide with shock and her eyes became concerned.

She was an attractive woman; not the type he went for; but the kind that George might take a liking to. A caring, intelligent, fast acting woman.

"Give me a hand!" Norton said. A moment later the two of them had Kayne in the bathroom. As she examined and cleaned the wound, Norton explained what had happened in short, quick sentences.

His mind, wasn't really on what he was saying or doing any more. He was, instead, attempting to decide what had to be done. Kayne should see a doctor. And the police—they had to be brought in one way or the other.

But would they act? Were they honest or crooked?

Norton wasn't stupid enough to believe that Delcado didn't own some very important and powerful people. In fact, maybe some of them owned Delcado. He didn't get his power from thin air.

He wondered: What about the police? Nobody would believe his story. The shooting part...but Delcado would be able to blame that on Williams, if he wanted to. They could say it was an accident. A hundred excuses. There would be no way of proving differently. Manny would back Delcado. And having been Kayne's agent, it would look good in the eyes of the authorities. The attack had, technically, been from Norton's and Kayne's end, not the other way around. As far as the clubs were concerned, that would be his word against theirs. He had a choice of just a few possible lines of action to take. One: go to the police. But what could he say to them

141

that they would believe? Nothing!

Run: Where?

Mexico?

Any place wouldn't be far enough to get away from Delcado's insane arm. And he'd have to get Norton and Kayne out of the way in order to ever open his clubs. Or just as an example. A powerful statement to anybody else who might try to get out of line. In fact, their lives were scratched—they'd be killed outright.

Delcado would see to it that.

Maybe he was over dramatizing the whole thing? Maybe if he went back and...begged? For what? A life under the thumb of a man like Delcado? He now saw what that kind of life could be. Jump when he was told to jump. Sit. Talk. Shut up. Become another terrified Manny Anson who seemed to have power but who was only a front man for the real powers. Manny Anson, who stopped talking when Delcado snapped his fingers. Who could just as easily stop living if Delcado clapped his hands.

And for what? Money? Fame? Power?

They weren't worth it.

Nothing was worth that kind of life.

Even if Delcado were a great guy, it wouldn't be worth it.

Norton only wished he had known that fact earlier that morning. But things had all seemed so different then.

The last couple of years had clouded his judgment. Dulled his senses. Two years of: cheap hotel rooms, whores, booze. Escaping failure. At least he wasn't dead. He'd had his life; his freedom. And he didn't know it. He had blown things! He had acted exactly as these bastards had expected.

Norton felt like a damned fool.

Just give him the chance to get that freedom again. Things would be different. He wouldn't need show business. Anything would be good enough. Just as long as it was honest.

And. With Esther Vivian! Esther!

He had almost forgotten her in the fury of the last hour. But she was what counted now.

That changed everything.

And that was silly. Fantastic. Impossible. Deliciously meaningful. It was a purpose for existing.

He'd just met her.

Yet, maybe she was just a symbol. An ideal. A goal. Something that he needed to aim for so that he would have the guts to face what was ahead.

Before it had been his silly career. A meaningless act without any purpose other than satisfying a weak ego and childish need for the admiration of as many women as he could get into bed. He'd been a damned bloody fool! Selling his life for mere ego strokes, fame and what? And it had all been stripped away by these power brokers who like to buy and sell people as if they were lifeless dummies. They were all just bodies that had sold out for a quick ticket to the easy life.

Well, things had to change. Somehow he had to get out from under and escape with his life.

Now he had a greater motive for living.

Esther Vivian's image shimmered into his mental vision and all he wanted to do was pull her into his arms and run away to some safe haven where they could spend their lives together. It was a fantasy, but something to hold on to, to desperately cling to. He needed that—in order to have the guts to face what was now so brutally ahead.

Face what he now knew he had to do.

There was no escape, just running until they caught up with him. He'd done enough running the past months to last him for the rest of his life. But that was nothing like it would be now, if he were running from Delcado's men.

The reason: simple! Because then he'd also be running from himself, too—Delcado and himself. The one—he could possibly take. But the second— no!

And nothing without the dream fantasy of walking through life with Esther—or some one like her.

The only chance he had was to face it now. Fight it now. While the time and the place were more in his control. He knew where they were, but they didn't know where he was. That was the only momentary advantage he had—and that couldn't last very long.

All the facts were there just to be gathered up like a deck of cards scattered on the floor. He had only to go out and seek them. Find them. Use them. Now was the only time he had to attack. He might even win. With Lilly to help. With the fact that Kayne was hurt. Maybe force Williams to tell a few facts. Use his limited knowledge about the two clubs, which, no doubt, had the gambling devices built in—or at least Delcado had the devices stored away somewhere. If he could find them! Find them, use the facts that he had against Delcado there might be a chance. Limited though it was. He must work with what they had. And maybe get enough facts against the man to bring an end to his activities. And redeem the blackballed condition of his own career in show business. That was an added possibility. But he needed as much help as he could get.

A plan started to jell in his mind. Vaguely at first, then slowly rounding itself out.

All they'd need would be a sexy girl with a little talent...Esther? If she really had talent! No. Not her. Not unless necessary. She was the possible reward if he succeeded—not the device to get that escape from Delcado's clutches.

Maybe he was only rationalizing? Maybe there was another way out? Maybe he was just tired of running? Maybe he just wanted to go out like a hero?

That was melodramatic.

But it didn't matter any more. The reasons didn't really count. They were just excuses. They gave his conscious mind something to focus on— and to hell with his subconscious mind!

He'd just been pushed around enough. And now, for the first time it was going to be Jamie Norton who pushed. And pushed hard. He might go out the loser but he was going to take a slice of meat out for himself. Even if it killed him.

For the first time he realized that he wasn't going out half-cocked. No real emotional fury. No temper—just cold-blooded reasoning. Plans. Motives. Reward. He had them all. Kayne would be in good hands here with Frankie. He could leave the guy with the knowledge that he'd be safe.

All he had to do was leave. Start. Where? Lilly. Lilly Benton. She knew more about Delcado's activities than he did. She might be scared but he thought that she would help him...Scared or not!

But Lilly was at Delcado's place. He'd have to find someway to get her out of there. Contact her by phone. Have her meet him some place. There they could figure things out. She was sure to help. She had to help.

But he couldn't call. His voice was known. It might be connected. He didn't want Frankie to know what he was about to do. If she found out there was no way of knowing what she might do. But who else would call? Who could call?

Esther?

Not her. He didn't want her to be involved. But would it be getting her involved? Actually nobody knew her. There would be no way of tracing her. She'd just be a voice on the phone.

Maybe that would be safe.

Maybe he could hold her once again in his arms before all hell broke loose.

☙ FOURTEEN ☙

Esther was dreaming about Norton when he started to frantically knock on her door. Vaguely her mind heard the sound. She wanted to keep hold of the dream image of his strong, naked body holding her tightly in his arms. But it simply started to fade. She desperately clung to the image of the man holding her so close. She didn't want him to stop making love to her. She felt herself squirming against him, nervously seeking a tighter union with that hungry body that was pressing harder and more violently against her. Oh, how delicious he felt. How she never wanted him to let her go. She simply didn't care about anything other than the wonderful sensation of this man in her arms. His fingers were caressing her breasts and his mouth circling downwards toward her neck and shoulders downward to her full bust line. The convulsive desperation of her body forced his lips hard against her and she felt the jerking moistness of his tongue as it ran along her flesh…and then faded to nothingness.

The dream lifted up with a throbbing sense of reality as the pounding sound outside shattered her sleep. At first she was confused, lying there in bed, half-asleep. The dream was still so sharply focused.

Then the pounding on her door shattered dreamland. She heard it from out of a foggy mist. The darkness was slowly beginning to thin. Then it took shape and form.

She was sitting up in bed, looking across the room through the open door into the front room.

Why didn't Ruthie use her key? The knocking continued.

"Oh, maybe she forgot it," she sighed out loud to herself as she slowly got up out of bed.

"Be right there!" she called.

"I don't see why you don't remember to bring your key, Ruthie!" she scolded, opening the door.

There was a breathless moment while she stood still. She felt her face flushing red.

The man just looked at her, his expression pleasantly surprised. At first she didn't recognize him. All she could think of was that she was naked as the day she was born and there was a man standing at the front door.

Then she moved. And even as she ran through the front room towards her bed she was mentally recognizing the man. It took all that time for her to recover her shock. Norton.

Jamie Norton!

What was he doing here at this late hour? And why?

She heard the door close and a man's footsteps.

Frantically she reached for her blue robe that was in the closet. After quickly wrapping it around her body she returned to the front room.

"What are you doing here at this hour?" she cried, almost angrily. The shock of having been found naked answering the front door was still wildly churning her emotions. "I thought you were my roommate, Ruthie."

"You always greet her that way?" he chuckled, then instantly became deathly serious.

She said, without thinking: "Oh…never mind!"

Then she looked carefully at the man, seeing details her embarrassment had blurred. The tight, drawn look in his eyes made her suddenly aware that something was wrong.

He was saying: "I don't have much time. I'm terribly sorry about this, but you were the only one I could turn to right now. Things are moving too fast. You're the only one that can help me right now."

"Sure, what is it?" She pulled the robe tighter around her and knotted the strap. The embarrassment had now completely left her.

"I don't have the time to explain everything, but believe me, this is a matter of life and death! I'm quite serious about that!"

She felt her heart pounding faster. They hardly knew each other and he was coming to her for help in a matter of "life and death!"

She felt terror. Sudden fear.

"Will you make a phone call for me?"

"Sure. Anything."

Her mind was racing, trying to figure out what all this meant. It was happening too fast and her brain was still a little foggy from sleep. What kind of trouble was she getting herself into? After all, she really didn't know this man. She wanted to know him. She wanted to discover he was everything she might imagine in a life-long lover. But that was childish, romantic fantasy. This was real life.

He might be in trouble with the law.

Then she realized that that didn't really make

any difference. There was something about the two of them that attracted each other. Something magical. And that's what counted. Both mentally and physically. It didn't matter to her if he was in any kind of trouble. If she could help that's all that counted. She would do anything for him. That realization stunned her—but was accepted very cool-headedly.

"You have a drink?" he asked.

"Whiskey."

"Great. Just a short one."

She led him to the kitchen, opened the cupboard and handed him the bottle.

"Help yourself," she offered. After giving him a glass she sat at the little breakfast table. "Now, tell me exactly what I can do for you."

He poured a strong, stiff drink and downed it in one gulp. It made her wince just to watch it. Then he turned toward her. His eyes were almost tragic looking. His mouth drooping. "I hate like hell getting you into this...and I don't have time for the details. But this much I can say. Delcado's in the rackets—"

"Delcado?"

"The guy giving the Big Party tonight. He's after *my* hide and if he gets it, God only knows what he'll do. There's only one way out. Get to him first."

"I don't see what you mean."

"Simple. There are certain people and certain facts we need...If I can get some of those facts, maybe I can get the law to take action against Delcado."

The man was being disconnected, incomplete. She didn't understand.

150

It didn't make sense. If there was some way to get at such a Delcado, then it seemed that the law would have done so a long time ago. "What can you do?"

"I can't explain now. Take my word for it! I know what I'm doing."

"What about the law?"

"No good. They wouldn't believe anything that I told them,

"Why?"

"It's too evolved to go into. Just believe me!" He looked seriously across at her. "You'll help?"

She would. Even though she couldn't help but think he was on the wrong track. Maybe the man was just drunk. Anyway, what was it to her? She had only known him for a couple of hours. "What do you want me to do?"

"Just call Lilly Benton for me."

Call Lilly Benton! That one jolted her right to the core. The nerve of him! Asking her to call the competition. Up to that point Esther held the fantasy that Norton might be truly interested in her. Now she wondered just what kind of fool she had turned into.

She suddenly felt cheap and almost dirty.

"You gotta be kidding!" Esther stated, coldly.

"She's the only one who can help. She knows things I don't know. I have to start somewhere and this is the only place I know where to start."

"Then what?"

"You call her, get her on the phone and then I talk to her."

"How will I get her on the phone? Why would she answer for me?"

From the way his eyes made a double take she realized that he hadn't thought things out that far. He sat there for a long time. His face expressionless. Not moving. Just looking past her. His eyes seemed to be searching. Seeking the answer to that question.

* * * * * *

From the moment Norton had left Frankie's to the time when he started for the meeting place which he had decided on, the incidents seemed to crowd into a series of impressions. Certain things stood out like splotches of color against the gray. One—was telling Frankie that he'd be leaving. "I'll either return or call in a few hours. You can take care of George, can't you?"

"Sure. But where are you going?"

"Never mind that. Just promise you won't call the police. At least for twelve hours."

She stood there before him, just looking blandly. "What do you mean?"

"Well, if I don't get in touch with you by then, I'll probably be dead. But don't call before then!"

Then the drive to Esther's.

Then Esther asked the million-dollar question. It wouldn't be easy getting Lilly on the phone. He had to think of something that only the two of them knew about. Use that as a key word or pass word. He had to think back. Somehow figure out a way to make her know that he was the one trying to get in touch with her.

Then he thought of one thing that might get Lilly to the phone. Something only the two of them, Esther and Kayne knew about. Esther. The blonde-

152

haired girl who spilled a drink on Norton's jacket. "I'll tell you what. Just say that you're the girl who spills drinks. I think she'll understand what that means. She got pretty mad about that. I'm sure that she'll put two and two together and figure I'm trying to get in touch with her. Anyway, it's the only thing I can think of right now."

He then suddenly realized he didn't know the number, There was no phone number. "Call information."

The phone was unlisted.

"Now what?" Esther asked.

That was a good question. Kayne might know. If he was conscious...

He called Frankie. Kayne was still unconscious. "Look through his jacket. Pockets. Wallet."

A moment later she returned to the phone. There wasn't any number that might have been Delcado's.

He hung up. "No dice!"

"It's important, isn't it?" she asked.

"Very. Very important!"

"Then why couldn't I go to the Delcado place and see Miss Benton personally. Nobody really knows me there. If the party is still going on..."

"It would be. That's an all night, all weekend type party."

"Then nobody would see me."

"Too dangerous." It was a good idea he realized, but he didn't see any reason to get Esther involved in that way. "No!"

"Yes! Why not? It'd be perfectly safe."

"No!" This was getting completely out of line. There was no reason to push things too far. Yet, the whole idea was to move fast before Delcado was able to find him. The man didn't know about Frankie or Esther. At those places—at least for a short time—they would be safe. But if the man made any kind of real search there was no reason that he couldn't discover Frankie. It would take time but it was highly possible for them to find out that Kayne had dated Frankie. And just under normal investigation they could track down every possibility until they were found Frankie's apartment. Maybe it wasn't as bad as he wanted to think, but he didn't have any desire to wait around and find out. Face the problem now. Force it to a conclusion.

"Well, I'm ready!" Esther's bright voice interrupted his thought. Esther was fully dressed in an evening gown. Blue and lacy. Fitting over her figure like a layer of sky had been painted on her. The sight was the most beautiful thing he'd seen.

"What the hell?" he snapped out of the spell and back to reality. "No! I won't let you get involved. It's too dangerous."

"I'm going to help. There's nothing you can do about it. I'll help, or call the police. And there's no danger. None at all. The only thing I'll do is find Miss Benton, and then tell her whatever you want her to know. It'll be as simple as that. Nobody knows me. There's no reason that I'd attract the least amount of attention."

"That dress will."

"Not really. Remember that everybody else there is dressed in flashy clothes."

He nodded at that. Maybe because it was a good idea? Maybe he was just too tired, mentally, to think of a better one? He knew he shouldn't let her do it, but there just didn't seem any other way. It was a

154

solution and he didn't have time to discover or invent another one.

Now, exactly two hours after Ester had left for the Delcado Estate, he was parking his car outside the entrance of a restaurant where he and Lilly had spend a lot of their time together between work breaks. It was just outside of a movie lot.

The street was dark. Only murky shadows surrounded him.

Taking out a cigarette, he slowly lit it, took a deep drag and then got out of the car. He was just beginning to look at his watch to check the time when bleak darkness exploded into pain and deeper blackness. He didn't even get a chance to react, mentally, to this defiant invasion. The painful impact of some thing hit the back of his head. A moment later the entire world closed in around him, crushing out his conscious awareness.

* * * * * * *

Kayne felt himself slowly moving out of the pit. It opened before his eyes like the opening of a curtain on a stage. The color. The lights. The shapes. The forms. They all seemed blurred at first. Then they sharpened. Frankie's beautiful face before his eyes. Leaning over him. She smiled. Her eyes were sad looking but her lips smiled. "How are you?"

"I don't know exactly." He tried to raise himself. Pain shot through his right arm and shoulder. "I think I'm hurt!" he managed to say almost with a light laugh in his voice. "Where's Norton?"

"Gone."

He jerked up. The pain pulled him back onto the

bed again. *"When?* Where? How long ago?"

"A little after you got here." Her voice sounded worried. "I wanted to call a doctor. The police. He wouldn't let me."

Kayne thought that over. Knowing Norton it meant only one thing. "He called a little while ago. About an hour or so. I don't remember how long, for sure. Wanted the number of a Mr. Delcado. Thought you might have it."

"Oh, damn his stubborn hide. With that temper of his he'll get himself killed!" He struggled to get up. "Help me."

"No! You stay there."

"You don't understand. Norton's going to get himself killed for sure. We gotta do something."

"I wanted to call the police..."

"Yes. Do that. That's the only way to stop it. Call them. Say there's a murder about to be committed at the Delcado Estate. To hurry before it's too late!" He gave her the address and then lay back, exhausted, sweating, feeling the pain in his arm throb terribly.

All he could do now was pray that nothing happened before the police were there to stop it.

"Tell them it's a matter of life and death!" he called, half deliriously struggling to sit upright. He didn't want to fall asleep any more, yet he felt the ebbing pain slowly dropping a sheet of dismal grayness across his vision and awareness.

The last thing he heard before losing consciousness again was Frankie's voice saying, "Hurry, you got to hurry. It's a matter of life and death. Somebody's going to be killed if you don't..."

The voice faded to nothingness.

156

FIFTEEN

The party hadn't changed much. There wasn't any music like before but Esther couldn't see anything else that had changed except that some of the people weren't looking as fresh as they had earlier—but that was inevitable.

For the first time since beginning this assignment, she was beginning to feel a nervous excitement flutter through her stomach. Not that she was afraid. It was more like being thrilled. Scared. Like a person watching a horror movie or mystery. She couldn't really think of herself as being in any real danger. There wasn't any reason for anybody to know what she was up to or her connection with Norton.

The moment she had suggested that she do this for him, it had seemed much like a storybook. A thrill. Excitement. An adventure. No real danger. Just an impulsive sense of doing something that could easily be written in a book or on the movie screen.

This, in a way, was her first real-life acting part.

After Norton had finally given in and said that she could go through with her plan, as long as she was very careful, he had explained most of the details she needed to know. The general outline.

Hardly enough to show her exactly how dangerous this "mission" was. Then he'd surprised and startled her by handing her a .38 revolver. "You know how to use a gun?"

She had nodded, tight-lipped and slightly fearful.

"Then take it. If anything happens where you have to use it, do so."

It seemed like a scene from a melodrama. She couldn't help feeling that he was slightly influenced by some of the parts he had played in the pictures. The drama etched on his face. The features were tense. His lips drawn into a thin line.

"But I won't need it."

"I know you won't. But just in case. Only a precaution. He had forced her to take it. She put it in her purse, holding it with two nervous fingers as she carefully dropped it into her bag.

Now she had to find Lilly Benton.

She saw a steward and walked up to him.

"You know where Miss Benton is?" she asked in a light, airy voice.

The man looked at her for a long time. Then he smiled. His eyes had become frozen at the dip between her breasts, at the bottom of her v-shaped neckline.

"I don't know for sure but I think I saw her go to her room some time ago."

"You know where that is?"

"Up the stairs, down the end of the hall. Last door." She started in that direction. At the bottom of the staircase she turned to see if anybody was looking in her direction. Nobody. The man she'd just talked to was walking towards another part of the house. He wasn't even paying any attention to her.

She quickly moved up the stairs, down the hall, to the door. She knocked.

Nobody answered.

She knocked again. "Miss Benton, are you there?"

A voice called.

It was muffled.

"Miss Benton?"

"Yes?" she heard a woman answer.

"It's important. I have to talk to you. Can I come in?"

"What about?"

"Believe me. It's important!"

"Okay." She heard footsteps and then the door opened.

"What is it?" Lilly Benton asked, trying to hide her face. She couldn't keep Esther from seeing the swollen bruise over her left check. The eye was blackened. Her lips were cut and puffy.

"You alone?" Esther asked, starting to move forward.

"Yes, what is it?" The tone was irritated.

"It's from Jamie. Jamie Norton."

Lilly let her in. Closed the door behind her. Then she turned.

"What is it?" Her hand moved up to her cheek, unconsciously touching the black mark there. "Is he all right?"

"Yes. He has to see you. It's important."

"They'd kill me." She leaned back against the door for support. "That bastard had this done to me just for telling Norton about...about, what I did tell him. They said they'd kill me, next time."

"You gotta go to him. It's important."

"Why?"

"He wouldn't tell me everything. But he thought that you could help him."

"What a fool. He doesn't know what he's up against. He doesn't have the least idea. They'll kill him. They're just waiting until he…"

"But he's depending on you to meet him at Santa Monica and Formosa. At the…"

The door pushed inward then, knocking Lilly off her feet. A small, heavyset man stepped in, followed by a huge, bloated giant of a man.

"Thank you, girls!" the shorter of the men said, "that's what we wanted to know!"

"Take a couple of the boys, Williams, and go get him. Bring him back. Into my private office. Use the back entrance. I want to see him personally" the taller man ordered. "Now, as for you ladies…"

Esther pulled the gun from her handbag and pointed it at the two men.

"What's this?" the man called Williams cried in mock alarm. "A spitfire"

"Stay where you are!" Esther ordered. She felt stiff and sick inside. She knew she wouldn't be able to use the gun. It was only a bluff but she had to make it good.

Dramatically she pulled back the hammer. From what little she knew about guns she realized that this wasn't necessary, but felt it would look good and maybe hold them back. It did hold Delcado back. It was Williams who moved forward.

The man's face was white with fury. "Give it to me, you little bitch!" he snapped, holding out his hand. "You won't use that on anybody. You know

160

that! Just hand it over!"

A sob was working up through Esther's throat. It was fear. Self disgust. Terror. Anger. A lumpy sickness was slowly moving from the bottom of her stomach up through her chest and throat. A hard lump of fear and terror.

For the first time she realized just what she had gotten herself into. She realized the seriousness of it. This was a life and death struggle. Yet, she couldn't pull the trigger.

Out of the corner of her eye she saw Williams make a blurring movement. His hand moved from his side to the inside of his jacket. It came out with a gun. "Okay, little lady, drop it."

Her eyes opened. At first she thought she was alone then she heard light but fast breathing. She turned and a surprised scream uttered from her startled lips.

Williams was moving closer. He reached for her.

She tried to get away but it was impossible. He was too fast. He rammed a fist into her face.

She heard voices, one said: "Take her in there!"

The world spun and she felt herself being laid backwards on the bed.

"You're a beauty!" a coarse voice muttered.

Through the daze she was aware of a man's hands stripping her body of all clothing and then as his fingers started exploring roughly the curving nakedness of her figure she felt the sickness return and then another scream shot past her trembling lips.

The stinging blow of his hand across her face didn't stop the frantic yell rasping through her lungs as she struggled to be free of him. Her fists smashed

161

at his body and face.

She screamed once more and then finding it possible to slip out from his slightly dazed and bleeding form, she moved off the bed and dashed across the room.

The door opened and Lilly Benton rushed in.

"You dirty, no good son-of-a-bitch! Damned bastard!" the actress screamed rushing toward him. "Leave the girl alone!"

Delcado's voice sounded behind her. "Okay, Williams. Get out! I want Norton."

Williams looked furiously at Esther, then Lilly and finally directed his eyes toward Delcado, that slob can wait!"

"You can wait. If you want your women, do it on your own time." The tight look in the gangster's eyes was enough to silence another word from Williams. The man quickly dressed and left.

Delcado followed the man out after a long, interested look at Esther's naked body.

Lilly stepped over to Esther and the young girl moved into her arms, sobbing.

Esther's whole body was shaking. Her mind retreated into an emotional shell. Time seemed to flash by her in a series of no movement and no shape or color or form or sound.

She was too sick to even think.

She heard the door close after a long time.

Her eyes opened. She was lying on the bed, fully clothed and alone. The door made a clicking sound and she realized that she was a prisoner.

* * * * * * *

Norton felt himself fighting through a fog, struggling to regain consciousness. He didn't know where he was. What had happened last? He couldn't remember anything, at first.

He knew it was very important to regain consciousness.

Then he began remembering why it was so important.

Where had things gone wrong?

"I see the bum is coming to. That's good."

The voice came out of the darkness. He didn't know from what direction, but he recognized it as Williams'!

"Wake up!" A hand slapped across his face. "Wake up, Mister Dead Man!"

The hand hit him powerfully once more.

Light, shape, form popped into existence. He was sitting in the back seat of a car. They were driving along a country road. He recognized it as a road on the Delcado Estate. He turned his head.

Williams was sitting at his right, a gun in his hand.

"I see our little pigeon has awakened," the man announced

"Go to hell!"

His remark was rewarded with the back of Williams' hand smashing across his face. His head snapped back. His whole face felt numb. Then moisture moved into his mouth. Blood.

"You keep in line or the next time I'll really work you over, but good!"

If only he had a gun then, he thought, he'd kill Williams. Regardless of the risk. One thing that he had promised himself: if he got the chance he would blow the god damned bastard's brains out!

The car pulled around to the back of the huge Delcado house. Then it stopped. The driver got out and walked around to Norton's side of the car, opened the door and indicated for him to get out.

"Move, bum!" Williams ordered, jamming the gun barrel painfully into Norton's side

He moved. A few moments later he found himself ushered into the private office of Delcado from a back entrance.

The big man was sitting down in his easy chair, smoking a cigar. A drink on the arm next to him.

He looked up as Norton came opposite him. "Well, now, how are things?"

The bastard!

"Get Manny and the two ladies!" Delcado ordered Williams.

The man left through the front entrance leading into the hallway.

"You know, you made a mistake sending that nice girl here. A very big mistake." Delcado shook the cigar back and forth in front of him. "She's such a nice young lady. But not much of a gun-moll."

"What've you done with her?" Norton demanded, feeling suddenly sick. "What the hell have you done with her?"

"Just relax. Have a drink. Take it easy."

Norton took a step in Delcado's direction. One of the men that had brought him there reached out and held Norton back. "Do as the man says. Have a drink."

Norton walked over to the bar, took a bottle of Scotch and poured himself a strong shot, then turned toward Delcado. "What you plan on doing with us?"

164

"I should think you'd know by now." Delcado didn't even turn in his direction, but his voice was calm, almost friendly sounding.

"You're a goddamned bastard!"

One of the men moved threateningly to him.

"Let him have his fun. Words don't hurt!" Delcado ordered. "Come on over here where I can see you!"

"Do as the man says!"

Norton did.

"What are you going to do with Esther?" Norton's hand gripped the glass violently until the knuckles whitened.

"What do you think?"

"Let her go!"

"Now, be realistic. I can't do that!"

The glass and its contents flew across the air between him and Delcado. He wasn't even aware of having thrown it.

It just missed the man's head by inches. The contents spilled over his jacket and shirt.

The calm expression changed to red violence.

Norton was about to leap forward at Delcado when a gun barrel slashed across the back of his head.

With effort he remained standing. The blow was staggering. But in his state of mind it didn't hurt as much as it should have. It only stunned him. Blackness started to cloud around his vision, but it cleared before it thickened any more.

He heard Esther's voice cry out in alarm, then he felt her clutching hold of him.

"Are you all right?" she asked.

For a moment he couldn't focus his vision on

her. Then he saw her delicate, beautiful features.

"God! What have I gotten you into?" he cried miserably.

"Cut the crap!" Delcado ordered. "Get that woman away from him. I want to say a few words to our over tempered man here!"

Esther was roughly brushed to one side.

Delcado loomed over him.

"You, mister would-be-hero, are about to see what becomes of people who try crossing Mr. Delcado. You learn your lesson real good!"

"Oh, for God's sake, let the guy have another chance!" Manny Anson's voice cried.

"You, Mister Agent-man, shut up!"

"Let me have this bum for just a few minutes!" Williams begged, moving up next to Delcado.

"Time enough for that. Right now I have a few things to say to this slob!" The man's face was slightly discolored. The features twisted in an ugly grimace.

"You little man with the hot temper," Delcado continued, tapping his finger on Norton's chest, "made just one mistake. You're as good as dead right now! I set you up for a good deal and then you slap my face. What's with you arty guys? You crazy or something? You get a sweet-smelling, money-making setup and you blow it, just like that! You blow it, but good!"

Norton was thinking fast. He had to do something to get Esther out of this. He had to do anything. Beg. Plead. Anything. There was no reason for her getting hurt. No reason to cause her harm.

"Look, Delcado. I'll go in for your deal. I'll leave the country. I'll do anything you want. Just let the girl out. Let her walk out unharmed and I'll be your man."

"Too late! You blew any chance you might have had earlier. Nobody, but nobody threatens Delcado with nothing—and gets away with it." He turned to Williams. "Then you know what the little actor-man did? He tried to hit me with a glass of my own Scotch." Without any pre-warning his arm swung around, clipping Norton full on the face.

His head jerked to one side. It felt as if every nerve and muscle had been ripped away from his body. Somehow be managed to keep from losing his balance.

"You see, Mister Actor-man, nobody does that to me and gets away with it. You're dead. You're all dead!" Delcado indicated both Norton and Esther.

That's when an unexpected voice spoke up from an unexpected direction.

"I have a surprise for all of you!" It was Williams that spoke this time. "All of you die—but for a different reason than you might think!" Everybody turned in the man's direction. He was holding a small revolver—and it was pointed in Delcado's direction. "You see, Mr. Delcado, the big boys don't like your operations—they don't want to see any gambling bit going on here in town...so they decided that they'd put somebody else in charge."

"What's the meaning of this?" Delcado roared, stepping threateningly forward.

"Just that you're a dead man!"

Now it was Williams' turn to be surprised because another unexpected voice broke into the conversation. It was just as deadly and just as harsh.

Mable.

She had just walked into the room. One look in her direction and both Lilly and Esther screamed. The woman's face had a long bloody cut running down the left cheek. Her arms were cut and still caked with red. The insane look in her eyes was enough to make everybody take a step backwards. The expression on her face was gnarled up into a horrible distortion of what he had seen of her earlier.

"I wouldn't do that if I were you!" she screamed.

Lilly moved in the girl's direction. Then they all saw at once that small gun in her hand. It was pointed in Delcado's direction.

"Where'd she get that?" Delcado demanded.

Mable just smiled. "Lilly's room."

"What you gonna do?" Manny cried in alarm.

"Kill these two...two slobs that did this to me!" she cried, pointing to the mutilation of her face.

Norton turned toward Delcado. He felt sick, horrible disgust.

"You bastard!" he yelled, starting to take a step toward the man.

Williams moved forward, ignoring the gun in Mable's hand. "Hold on, Mister Norton!"

Then he turned suddenly and fired on the girl without warning. And that's when Norton jumped him. It was impulsive, but all the hate and violence and sickness and all of the horror of what these people had done to others and himself abruptly exploded. His hand shot forward hitting Williams arm, jerking him around while at the same time slashing a fist into the man's face.

Williams staggered backwards. A groan of sur-

168

BODIES 4 SALE, BY CHARLES NUETZEL

prise sounded from his bleeding lips. He raised his
arm in front of his face to protect it from another
blow. The only trouble was—Norton sent his other
fist into the man's stomach. A rabbit punch on the
back of the neck smashed Williams to the floor.
There he remained, groaning in pain, but not moving.

Norton turned, reaching for where he had seen
the gun fall. It wasn't there.

"This what you looking for?" Delcado asked,
leveling the weapon at Norton.

What had happened to Lilly? Norton wondered
as he leaped toward the bigger man.

He wasn't fast enough. Delcado fired the gun
and he felt a searing pain erupt in his side. It burned
as if a red-hot sword had ripped straight through
him. For a moment he thought he would black out,
but his mind cleared.

It was as if he were watching the scene from a
theater seat. Detached from his body. As if he controlled what was happening on the screen.

The gunshot had not stopped his forward
movement towards the other man.

His fists rammed into Delcado's stomach. The
big man doubled over.

One of his hands fumbled for the gun as another
bullet fired again. Then he twisted the weapon out
of the slack fingers of the mobster.

Things had happened so fast that everybody else
in the room had been paralyzed. The only actors had
been Lilly, Norton, Williams and Delcado.

Williams was still groaning on the floor.

Mable was lying on the floor—dead.

Norton was turning around, the gun in his hand.

169

He aimed it at the two strong-arm men who were just starting to move into action.

They froze.

Delcado slumped to the floor, his face white. His eyes open, a trickle of red started to drool from his lips.

There was a widening bloody blotch starting to spread on his chest where the second bullet had gone.

"Okay, just stay where you are, everybody."

"I have them covered with the other gun," Esther said from behind him.

"Lilly?"

"I'm...okay..." The voice was thin and faraway.

"She's hurt. Badly," Manny said.

"It's nothing, really darling, just a...wound in the.... I'm all right. Really!"

"Okay, you two mugs," Norton snapped, motioning the other two men back against the wall. "Make one move and you're dead."

"Esther go to the phone and call the police."

She walked over to the desk and was just reaching for the telephone when the huge double doors burst open and half a dozen men crowded into the room.

"Now that's the fastest service I've ever seen," Norton laughed, beginning to feel the after effects of the wound he'd received. "The damnedest... damnedest service I've...ever..."

The world was spinning. He was at the bottom of a whirlpool which was sucking him upward into an infinity of endless black space.

♈ EPILOG ♈

It was a private party. In the private home of Lilly Benton, famous star of television and movie screens.

Those present belonged to a private club. Entrance requirements: wounded or involved with certain dramatic true-life events.

Those present:

Mr. and Mrs. George Kayne.

Jamie Norton, one-time big star of movie and television and record.

Miss Esther Vivian. One-time small-town girl, struggling starlet.

Event: A celebration.

George Kayne was speaking, holding up a glass of champagne. "I wish to make a toast at this point, if I may..."

The others clapped their hands.

Kayne's voice was slightly thick. Nobody noticed. He almost seemed to sway slightly. Nobody noticed.

"To Norton, Kayne and Vivian!"

They didn't wait. All downed their drinks.

Norton leaned toward Mrs. Kayne. "Well, Frankie, how's it feel to be married to a future famous piano-man who likes to blow a little song now

171

and then."

She just smiled knowingly. Swallowed her drink and turned to her husband.

Lilly spoke up. "Well, when is the happy event going to take place?"

Norton turned toward her.

"I'm speaking to you, Jamie."

"Me?"

"About what?"

"Well...if you don't know...maybe I'd better not tell you!"

She laughed.

Esther nudged Norton under the table, smiling sweetly.

"You know," Kayne said, beginning to get thoughtful, "every time I think about what happened...it shakes me up."

"Oh let's not talk about it" Esther cried desperately, attempting to break the conversation off. "Every time we get together it all comes up—"

"Hell, darling, it's the only thing any of us have done that is really adventurous. I mean, real-life adventures. We all turned out heroes!"

"Heroes, shmeroes!" Kayne snorted. "Who cares? I came close enough to adventure to do me for the rest of my life. Never again!"

"Oh, can't we talk about something more interesting?" Esther pleaded.

"Okay," Kayne exploded, turning to Frankie, "Tell us, from the viewpoint of a disinterested bystander, what do you think of our act?"

"Norton, Kayne and Vivian?" Frankie's face looked mock-serious. She tapped her chin with a finger, thinking hard. "Well, I really don't know.

Now this Norton guy. He...well, those gags. Right out of Cornsville."

"But the audience liked them." Lilly pointed out.

"The others quickly agreed.

"And then," continued Frankie, "there's the matter that—what do you call her?—The sexy part of the act!" Her hand went out claw-like toward Esther. She made a cat-like sound. "If I wasn't married to George I'd be jealous as hell!"

"You mustn't swear like that," Kayne scolded.

"Yes, dear." She looked demurely at her husband. "And as for that piano-man. And that singing! Horrible!" She laughed.

The others laughed.

Then Lilly turned toward Norton again. "Well, tell us. When is the happy event?"

Norton looked puzzled.

"Don't act like a sap! We're all waiting for the announcement."

"What announcement?" Kayne laughed. "He doesn't know?"

"You mean you didn't ask her yet?" Lilly inquired in surprise.

"What?"

Kayne stood and walked over to a corner of the room where there was a concert grand. He sat down behind it. Dramatically placed his fingers on the keyboard and started playing.

The wedding march.

Norton turned red-faced.

"Well?" Lilly asked.

Kayne returned. "You dumb or something?"

Norton turned to Esther. "Well, how about it?"

"What?" she asked, her face looking blank but her eyes sparkling anxiously.

She stubbornly set her jaw. "I don't know what in the world you're talking about. I want the whole thing. Lay it out. Right! Word for word!"

Everybody else was stone quiet. All listening. Hardly breathing. Their eyes excited and anxious.

"Will you marry me?"

Esther shook her head up and down. Her lips burst open, saying, "I thought you'd never ask!"

"You, and everybody else!" Kayne cried. "Congratulations!"

The others quickly agreed.

There was laughter. Norton was kissing Esther excitedly, almost passionately on the lips.

Only Lilly seemed slightly sad for a moment. But she quickly brightened up. Nobody would have noticed that her smile was forced, or that her eyes weren't misty from happiness.

"Well now," she said passing the champagne bottle around and raising her glass. "Well, darlings, all I can say is that I hope the marriage will be as much a success as the new act. Here's to Norton, Kayne and...and...Norton?"

☗ ABOUT THE AUTHOR ☗

Charles Nuetzel was born in San Francisco in 1934, and writes:

"As long as I can remember I wanted to be a writer. It was a dream I never thought would materialize. But with the help of Forrest J Ackerman, who became my agent, I managed to finally make it into print.

"I was lucky enough not only in selling my work to publishers but also ending up packaging books for some of them, and finally becoming a 'publisher' much like those who had bought my first novels. From there it as a simple leap to editing not only a sci-fi anthology, but a line of sci-fi books for Powell Sci-Fi back in the 1960s. Throughout these active professional years I had the chance to design some covers and do graphic cover layouts for pocket books & magazines."

Much of his work in covers and graphics are a result of having had a father who was a professional commercial artist, and who did a number of covers for sci-fi magazines in the 1950s and later for pocket books—even for some of Mr. Nuetzel's books.

In retirement he has become involved in swing dancing, a long time lover of Big Band jazz. But more interestingly world travels have taken him (and his wife Brigitte) across the world, to Hawaii, Caribbean, Mexico, Kenya, Egypt, Peru, having a life-long interest in ancient civilizations. His website is full of thousands of pictures taken during these trips.

www.ingramcontent.com/pod-product-compliance
Lightning Source LLC
Chambersburg PA
CBHW020335260626
47156CB00004B/1537